About the Author

Paul is an English-born writer of divergent genres of work, including satirical fiction, drama, poetry and recently, crime thrillers. He has produced illustrated satirical work and a satirical play. He grew up in a serious and academic family, his father a Czech-Jewish refugee. Paul, an English Literature and Linguistics Graduate from London University, runs a School of English in the town of Windsor where he currently lives.

Dedication

Thanks in particular go to my close friend Adrian Courtenay, whose belief in me has required no proof of success- just as well in such a capricious matter as writing novels!

P. Symonloe

THE DIRTY RASCAL

AUSTIN MACAULEY
PUBLISHERS LTD.

A CIP catalogue record for this title is available from the British Library.

ISBN (Paperback) 9781784559861
ISBN (Hardback) 9781784559878

www.austinmacauley.com

First Published (2015)
Austin Macauley Publishers Ltd.
25 Canada Square
Canary Wharf
London
E14 5LB

Printed and bound in Great Britain

I'm the King of the Castle and you're the Dirty Rascal!
(A traditional children's nursery rhyme)

Map of
Windsor and Eton

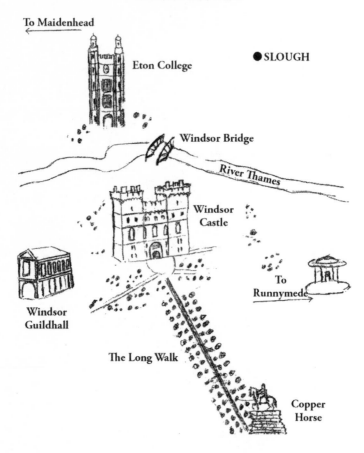

To Maidenhead

Eton College

● SLOUGH

Windsor Bridge

River Thames

Windsor Castle

Windsor Guildhall

To Runnymede

The Long Walk

Copper Horse

Chapter One

"OK, now we know who you both are."

He looked down again in thought for quite a time…

"So here's the thing. In fact the strangest thing and well… the most… let's say unnatural thing has occurred."

Superintendent George Pawley spoke on in a low watchful growl. The two detectives focused very intently on his words.

"In Slough this morning a… well… look, you need to get over there. Come back and tell me what in Christ's name happened to this poor creature. Bring me the details, but from what I've heard so far I don't know if I really want them. Christ this job gets harder as you start knocking on!"

Earlier that morning…

Lieutenant Zac Dolby was in his hotel bathroom shaving, pausing now and then to look across at the towering grey walls of Windsor Castle. The folk of the ancient castle-town were mostly still asleep in their duveted bedding or doing whatever English people do at 6am in the morning. He looked with interest at the turrets of the castle. Zac wondered if Her Royal Highness was up and about. Since landing at Heathrow Airport the previous evening his excitement at the thought of exploring this ever-so-English town had grown. He wanted to see what these Brits were like in the flesh. The Queen of England he thought, what would she be doing at this second, just a black crow's hop away behind the castle battlements? No matter for now. Important right now was an examination of the present facts of his life. The main fact was that he had been rudely transplanted from his native habitat into this Disney castle-town lookalike on a wet and grainy island thousands of miles from everything he knew. He figured though that Windsor was, like anywhere else – a seething, irrational, imperfect and thus normal kind of place. It was perhaps a cynical view for a personable young man. Zac, raised in a large Jewish tenement household in Brooklyn New York, sometimes felt as if he had Woody Allen on one shoulder and his mother on the other, giving him a stream of dry humorous "useful" advice. He looked again at the dizzyingly sheer walls of Windsor Castle. What dark happenings must have gone on in there and in this town over the centuries? It all piqued his curiosity more than a little. He looked at his watch. Heck, nearly time to meet his new English oppo. What was her name again? He plucked a small piece of paper from the odds and ends on the hotel bedroom table and exited the room.

"Urgent message sir…"

The hotel concierge just missed his target however as Zac crossed the lobby and headed out of the building.

Abbi Matilda, having stayed with friends the previous night in Maidenhead, a town some eight miles from Windsor along the River Thames, stepped off an early Slough to Windsor train, pulling a small suitcase on wheels. Soon she blended with the narrow old streets that led to wider old streets and the ancient buildings of Windsor. The quirky buildings were now occupied by the usual high street names. The made-over cobbled streets led to the modern-medieval heart of this 21st century fortress. Abbi felt that she didn't really belong to the picturesque castle-town. After two years working the gritty streets of Manchester, this little nugget of ancient history was foreign to her. Things felt just out of reach – just short of an in-the-moment experience. As an outsider of course she could make detached deductions. It was a skill that had brought her rapid promotion through The Force. She passed the tattooist's parlour and the hamburger outlet. In the latter sat a thick-set man with a face of simple brutality. Opposite him were a loud trashy woman and two shaven-headed kids fighting over a burger. The kids fed as she walked on. The parents maintained vague overfed stares across and beyond each other. Life was normal and the traffic inched over the sleeping policemen on the boutique-riddled streets of the quaint castle-town. Windsor Castle itself stood out in bold on the near skyline. What was this Yank's name again?

They were meeting in the mall at one of the numerous café-bars in a crude Italianate style, in which you could at almost any hour of the day buy: a bucket of foul brown liquid, a larger bucket of evil-looking liquid, or a bath-full of nauseating brown liquid.

Zac scanned the mall for anyone that might look like a female detective in the Thames Valley Police Force. As a detective himself, he figured this was an acid test for his powers of deduction. These Brits had created Sherlock Holmes, and fictional though he was, as an American cop Zac wanted to spot an English policewoman at fifty feet to show he was no rooky Yank. The unwritten rule of 'man arrives before woman' seemed to hold true as Zac waited. In twenty minutes he managed to guess wrongly five times that a series of professional looking women was his new colleague. He was just on the verge of being irked when a tap on his shoulder surprised him just enough to make him start.

"Mr Dolby?"

"Yes! Lieutenant Dolby. That is, Zac Dolby, hi."

Zac had to admit to himself that he had been about as wrong in his deductions of an English policewoman detective as it is possible to be. This was an aesthetic looking woman of some thirty years with a slender and sensual figure, long silky fair hair and intelligent green eyes. He was very pleased to meet his new partner in the business of crime.

"Have you been waiting long?"

"Heck, no ma'am, just showed up!"

Abbi looked sceptical at this, as she assessed this alien with inquisitive yet appreciative eyes. Well-constructed she concluded, without the grotesqueness of a body-builder.

"Oh OK, it's just that I spotted you here about ten minutes ago and thought I would just buy some chewing gum quickly before I introduced myself."

"Abbi Matilda, Thames Valley."

She held out a sleek feminine hand.

Zac replied untruthfully, avoiding her gaze.

"Yeah, I figured it was you."

Abbi gestured towards the café.

"Shall we get a coffee?"

"Sure thing."

She led him in.

"Let's hope it's drinkable. We don't want you to get a bad first impression."

On the inside they picked out some bored waiting staff speaking sort-of English. They were over-trained in vigorously cleaning the coffee-making machinery and surfaces, and under-trained in the arts of customer service and coffee-making. Abbi's discerning gaze scanned the interior of the Italianate café. It offered every variation except normal well-blended coffee with normal milk, slightly warm, but not foaming like the washing up.

"What can I get you ma'am?"

Zac's question gave away the noticeable politeness of an American abroad.

She looked again at the board for a more acceptable choice than brown fluid. She opted for a flavoured water tasting of Aspartame. Not looking at the menu, Zac chose a café latte.

"Gum?"

Zac looked with interest at the sleek female addition to his world.

"Yes, I've just given up smoking."

"Man, really? I just quit two weeks ago!"

They relaxed with this common bond. Conversation became more animated.

Abbi looked interested.

"How many?"

"A thirty-a-day Jones."

"A Jones?"

"A habit. A Jones is a habit."

"OK, so thirty?"

"Yeah, you?"

"Oh, fifteen max."

Something in Abbi's tone left Zac uncertain on this count.

"So lieutenant, when did you get in?"

Abbi pronounced this "*loo*-tenant" as distinct from "*lef*-tenant."

"Yesterday evening. It was that terminal where you take the subway to get back to civilization."

Abbi smiled.

"I figure I passed through two time zones just to pick up my trunk!"

Abbi laughed out loud at this.

"So, what do you think of us so far, lieutenant?"

Zac smiled again.

"I guess it's too early to say, ma'am."

"Keeping your powder dry, right?"

"Yeah I guess. I kinda like to observe first if you get me?"

Abbi did feel an affinity with this.

"You'll be a breath of fresh air at Division."

"How come?"

"Because most of the DI's are like Labradors with their tongues hanging out, if you know what I mean?"

"Eager you mean?"

"Well, that's part of it I suppose, but mainly for the usual reasons."

Zac laughed, feeling he should be able to get along fine with these Brits if he cut his deck right.

Abbi's mobile rang and rang off immediately. She looked down puzzled.

"Can't have been urgent."

She resumed eye contact with Zac.

"You from around these parts, Miss Matilda?"

"Call me Abbi, please."

Her cheek may have flushed fleetingly Zac thought, but he wasn't completely sure.

"I'm from a small village in Norfolk originally, but I've been working in Manchester for the past two years. I'm staying in a hotel here tonight. I feel strange in Windsor. It's so small and quaint. It feels a bit like living in a pretty biscuit tin."

"What happened with you? Why are you here?"

Zac looked thoughtful.

"Truth is, exactly one week ago from today I was at home in Brooklyn, minding my own business, watching the ballgame. Next thing I get this call from some top level schmo deciding my life for me. Was I pissed!"

"You didn't want to come here then?"

"Heck no. See I was doing real good in my job. I had a place, buddies, you know?"

Abbi looked sympathetic.

"You don't get asked in our job. They just dump you with stuff."

Zac exhaled.

"Too right! It's out of line."

"So why Windsor Mr Dolby?"

The American rolled his eyes quickly upwards.

"See, the thing is I'm really meant to be here sharing intelligence with your Metropolitan Police on inner-city crime in London, but they weren't ready for me."

"Why..."

Abbi's question was cut short by her mobile ringing again to the tune of "Ring-A-Ring O' Roses." Zac sat back. This working partnership was getting off to a pretty good start. Mentally he was preparing to tell Abbi more about his life back home. As luck had it, he didn't get the chance.

"Get your stuff lieutenant. We're in business. Back to the trains right now!"

Chapter Two

The train from Windsor took them to a connecting train in Slough, which passing through Maidenhead, took them on to Reading. Thames Valley Divisional Headquarters looked grim and grimy. Zac wasn't prepared for just how small-scale and disappointing some things were in England. Windsor was an historic jewel in a green crown of farms and countryside, but this... this was really pretty lamentable compared with the American version.

"Christ, a Yank!"

"Sir?"

"Sorry son, nothing personal!"

Having traipsed the dreary corridors of Thames Valley HQ, occasionally catching unnerving smells from the police canteen, Zac and Abbi now walked side by side into Chief Superintendent Pawley's cramped office. They sat down on the other side of his large desk. In fact the desk was absurdly large for the small drab office. Positioned at the corner of the desk was a large antique inkstand. Alongside was a family group photo that was probably the Chief Superintendent's family from some decades earlier.

"George Pawley."

The Chief Superintendent in the flesh held out a rigid hand and smiled an expansive, verging-on-scary, smile at them both.

"I'm rather old school I'm afraid!" he shouted, "But fair too I hope!"

Abbi and Zac stared back at him waiting for a sign as to why they had been summoned with such urgency to the centre of the Thames Valley Police universe.

"You a Yank too?"

Abbi looked straight ahead.

"No sir, I'm a Limey."

Pawley stopped short of his next sentence, to look Abbi up and down more searchingly. Then he looked down at the paperwork in front of him.

"DI Matilda isn't it? Thought I recognized the name. Your father was a bloody talented policeman. Is he still with us?"

"No sir, he's dead sir."

Pawley sighed.

"Sorry to hear that."

He straightened himself in his red leather chair deliberately and with an air of moving on gravely.

"OK, now we know who you both are."

He looked down again in thought for what seemed quite a time.

"So here's the thing. In fact the strangest thing and... well the most... unnatural thing has... occurred."

The transatlantic divide became suddenly very small in the cramped grey office with the over-sized desk, as George Pawley spoke on in a low watchful growl. The two detectives focused very intently on his words...

It was roughly half an hour from Reading to Slough by fast train. Abbi and Zac sat in a carriage on a journey punctuated by the conversation of some "suits," speaking in loud assertive voices about deals and closing. Two tall twenty-whatevers were talking about Ian and how he was a real tosser because promotion always went to bloody graduates, like him (Ian that is), rather than honest work-your-way-up-from-the-ground-floor guys, presumably like them. They would, of course, have traded places with this Ian the Tosser in a heartbeat, given half a chance.

Abbi raised her eyebrows in Zac's direction as if apologising for the English. Zac smiled.

"What's this Slough city like then?"

"It's not a city really."

Abbie scanned the middle-horizon for the two huge cooling towers on the distant industrial estate.

"More a town."

"Right."

Zac nodded deliberately.

"It's not pretty, but pretty useful for shopping and things."

Looking at Zac she could see that further information was needed.

"It's, well, an incredible ethnic mix really. It was industrial, now it's much more technology and the like. It was a place of very high employment in the fifties and sixties. It may still be today for all I know. Oh, and there are quite a few curry-houses. Are you into curry, lieutenant?"

Zac considered.

"I guess. Do you know any good ones?"

Abbi smiled. "I'll find one."

They looked away from each other at the passing assortment of discarded or forgotten items that occur along a railway line; sand stood in small heaps, tangled coils of cable, bricks grown over with hardy weeds, defiant against all that the droughts and floods had thrown at them. This all slid soundlessly past to the rhythmical beat of the train's progress. Abbi pointed across the parallel tracks as the train pulled into Slough.

"We'll go back on that train."

Abbi pointed to a siding reserved for the train that made the eternal shunt from Windsor to Slough, Slough to Windsor. It was about as simple a journey as you could get in the trembling web of train movements in Southeast England.

Zac toyed with his lapel, slightly tongue-tied.

The train pulled in. Their steps synchronised perfectly as they connected with the asphalt of the station platform.

"Where to now, Miss Matilda?"

"We need to get to a shopping centre called Queensmere. It's about five minutes on foot. Better get over there quickly. I really don't like the sound of this."

Zac saw something new in the slender English woman detective. She had a tone of resolve and a manner suggesting real strength of character. Her voice exhibited more than mere self-confidence. It suggested that whatever life threw at her, like it or not, she would see it through to the absolute end. Zac registered his liking for this as he hurried with her through the ticket barriers. He made his first footfall on the streets of Slough. They walked fast and mostly in silence. There was graveness between them, stemming from their meeting with George Pawley. If that old campaigner had been shaken by events then there was surely something to be feared here. They were in any case a few short minutes from the truth, whatever it turned out to be.

Zac broke the silence.

"Do we know what we're gonna see?"

Abbi looked over as they walked on hurriedly.

"Not exactly. We just know that it's spooked everyone involved. I believe it's something strange and what did Pawley say?"

"Unnatural"

"Yes, unnatural."

In a few short minutes they were approaching a clutch of uniformed officers at the edge of Queensmere Shopping Centre in the heart of Slough.

"Is this the mall?"

Zac's private assessment was that English shopping malls were kind of small.

"Yes this is it. Let's go in."

A number of journalists and photographers were stalking around like a group of big cats in the immediate area, making bored conversation, while all the time keenly eyeing the police tape to see who was coming and going.

They interrupted the detectives' progress with questions.

"Do you know what's in there sir, madam?"

Zac and Abbi walked past them silently.

"It is true that it isn't actually a human killing?"

Badges were flashed at the uniformed officers guarding the outer crime scene, with 'Police Do Not Cross' tape cordoning off the area to the general public. They made their way steadily along the concourse until reaching the rear of a hushed huddle of further uniformed police and Scene of Crime Officers at the crime-scene proper. There was muted conversation taking place as they edged closer.

"What's going on? Why are you two here?"

Abbi and Zac turned to be confronted by a tall fair-haired man with a Michael Douglas hairstyle, swept back over a narrow, rodent-like face. Very black eyes contrasted with the colour of his hair and complexion. He had clearly been on the scene for a while. The question came again.

"What are you up to? There's more than enough of us here as it is."

Abbi looked unemotionally at the assertive interrogator.

"None of yours, Wylie" she answered calmly.

"Anyway we could ask you the same question."

Before he could respond to this, and having all the while been inching their way past the Scene of Crime Offers, they were at the front. Wylie let them pass.

"OK, I suppose you'd better take a look now you're here."

At last they had come to the full fact of the scene. Zac was slightly in front of Abbi.

"Jeez that's a lot of blood."

Abbi nodded silently.

"As much as a man… This is horrible, really horrible."

She sounded agitated.

Wylie had turned around to face them.

"I'd say what we've got here is some kind of ritual act."

Zac was still taking in the scene.

"Man, this is way creepier than a human death… Did you see the blood? Have you questioned anyone yet, detective?"

Wylie fixed his eyes on Abbi rather than answer the American.

"No, but I will. There's a centre manager floating around somewhere apparently; I'll go and talk to him. I'm getting hold of the CCTV footage as well."

He paced off self-importantly.

Zac was still squinting at the scene.

"It's some kind of goose, right?"

To Abbi, Zac suddenly sounded very American.

"No, that is, or rather was, a Mute Swan, a possession of The Queen. She turned a grave look on him.

"This whole thing looks more ghastly by the minute."

Zac continued to stare.

"How the hell did it wind up like that?"

Abbi's eyes followed his line of sight.

The swan had been arranged in the form of an angel. Its wings had been pinned up together in a wide white arc. The head hung down on the paving slabs. It looked at once both beautiful and gruesome.

Zac was finding it hard work to speak aloud. Within the compass of the bloody scene everyone seemed frozen into silence. The swan had, by the look of the pool of congealing blood, been bled to death. The surrounding slab-stones of the shopping centre floor, now dazzling the eyes in a slanting sun, were a bright crimson. The poor creature had been butchered, but not as a conventional butcher would work. This action had been carried out in a very particular manner to produce a very particular effect. Away off to the left-hand side of the animal was an oddly antique-looking black object, metal by the look of it. A minute perhaps had passed by the time Zac noticed that Abbi was looking intently at the screen of her tablet, fished hurriedly from her bag.

"Christ," she breathed. "Shit."

She flushed briefly at her own instinctive swearing.

"What's up?"

Zac stood very close, just touching her elbow as he leaned in towards the screen. They stared together silently at the page.

"I thought I recognised something. I did medieval history as part of my degree. I knew there was something here that rang a bell. This has got to be the work of a nutcase... and a sadistic nutcase at that."

She sounded shaken.

"Look at this."

She scrolled down the page headed Medieval Instruments of Torture.

Zac pored over the page as she thumbed down to a particular one of the grizzly items under the main heading.

Zac started.

"You figure that..."

She cut him short.

"I do, in fact I'm certain of it."

"This poor creature was savaged by this..."

She fought for speech... this... instrument here."

Her fingers brushed the screen under the title: Breast Ripper. The illustration showed a pair of viciously sharpened tongues, like huge pincers, devised to rip flesh from the bone while the victim was still alive.

"Now look over there."

He followed her line of vision to a black metal object on the flag stones, still shining with wet blood.

As Zac peered over, his line of sight was obscured by DI Wylie's white-gloved hand waiving a small white piece of card at them.

"There was one other thing at the scene. This was found under one of the creature's wings."

Zac strained to see what was on the card. Wylie held it to his chest.

"What is it?"

Wylie was guarded.

"It's just a picture of a swan with blood down the front of its chest feeding some baby swans. I'd say this is the work of a very sick mind."

"Cygnets, Wylie," Abbi offered.

"Oh yes, I forgot you were educated before you got into The Force, DI Matilda; cygnets, then."

"You should have tried education yourself Wylie; it might have agreed with you."

"So did you see the centre manager?

"No, DI Matilda. He's not here at present, but I've set up an appointment with him at my office for tomorrow."

"They've given you an office have they? Well I saw them emptying the cleaning cupboard yesterday...so..."

Abbi smirked at Zac.

Wylie resisted the bait.

"Anyway I've got things to do. I'll leave you two to play detectives."

He walked off again. Then turning on his heel he came right back up to them: very close, without attitude and in earnest.

"I don't yet know what exactly, but I'm sure the picture's telling us something."

Zac took in the comment with a serious nod.

"Who first reported this?"

"The centre manager, lieutenant, according to SOCO. I'll slap him about a bit and extract a confession."

Zac ignored the sarcasm. He could see the Englishman was rattled and defensive.

Wylie grimaced, turned and finally left them.

Zac was part thrilled, part horrified.

"Man, what's all that about? And what's the picture about?"

Abbi shuddered.

"I really don't know. It's all too awful."

"Let's get back. There's nothing more we can do here for now. Let's leave the rest to SOCO and Wylie."

Zac nodded. They turned and headed back towards the train station.

Getting back to Windsor Central Railway Station, the sun was hovering over the statue of Queen Victoria, just beginning to lower its course in the late summer sky. They marched grimly back through the shaded passages of Windsor's old cobbled streets. This day was the first sun anyone had seen in a summer of floods and almost eternal glowering windy, raining weather. Up from the train station, along with Zac and

25

Abbi, came tourist throngs. They formed into shapes like weather systems, also coming up from the coach parks in ragged troughs of ample and loudly-dressed jollity. They looked up and observed the castle towering over the town doing its impervious and imperious detached routine. It looked on, gave nothing away, offered no clues to the insect mortals crawling round its base as to whether something of moment was about to happen, or if life was just taking another standard heartbeat in the billions during its watch. The castle didn't *do* surprise. It projected a sense of haughty and grey mystery. There was though, always a gasp or two of surprise in store for the meandering tourist groups spreading and developing in their mini weather-systems, grazing their way up towards Windsor High Street.

Zac spoke.

"You know Windsor feels kind of like a private club?"

Abbi looked questioningly at the American.

"Well that is, not in a bad way. Sorry I didn't mean to be impolite, ma'am."

"Don't worry lieutenant, I'm not offended. How do you mean though, a private club?"

Zac considered.

"I guess I mean you either belong or you don't. It makes me think of my neighbourhood back home. It doesn't seem to matter where you go, there's always some outfit that wants you on the outside if you know what I mean?"

"Yes, I do," Abbi returned simply. "I certainly don't belong here. Not yet anyway."

Zac wanted to know where they were headed.

"Are we going back to base, wherever that is?"

Abbi looked at her watch.

"Yes, better had. Base is Windsor Nick, but let's take five minutes by the river first. I need some air."

The mute swans glided noiselessly on the Thames close by. They walked by the river for some ten minutes, then up Thames Passage and into Thames Street in comfortable silence. They passed on through the lights and shades; past the numerous cafes and restaurants. Zac wondered if the visitors and tourists had taken in the more enigmatic clues to the town. He'd certainly noticed the mute signals of the townsfolk to each other – their wordless communication. These abstract facets to the town were easily the most revealing: the special atmosphere, the coded rituals. They were like wisps of smoke from secret fires, smouldering in the hearts and minds of the people. Zac figured they were difficult to interpret unless you were truly part of the joint. The castle held the answer. So too did the ancient cracked and crazed streets. If you wanted to know more you'd have to serve your time. Until then the drawbridge was up and you are on the wrong side. Remote, Zac thought. He was certainly outside the walls of the town's private club. Feeling very American, he turned to Abbi.

"You know that guy Wylie, right?"

Abbi looked straight ahead.

"Yes, but please let's not talk about him. We're due back at work soon. I've asked for a lift from Windsor to Reading Nick with Uniform. We've got to report back to Pawley. Come on, lieutenant."

Zac shrugged and accepted her silence on the matter of Wylie. Like the town itself, Abbi had her mysteries.

George Pawley welcomed them in with a confidential wave of the hand.

"How are you getting on, Lieutenant Dolby? DI Matilda looking after you?

"Yes sir, she sure is."

"Good. By the by, I've arranged for you to move into police digs. It's close to everything you'll need in Windsor and better than those antiseptic hotel bedrooms. Anyway let's get down to business."

A nervous tension showed its hand now as the subject on all their minds came back sharply into focus, in the small and dingy office with its oversized desk. George Pawley spoke first.

"I'll tell you what Wiley has come up with – which isn't much, – then maybe you two can give me your own findings on what happened in Slough. We know already that this poor creature was probably killed sacrificially. We surmise this from the amount of blood at the scene. It seems to be a ritual kind of blood-letting. Christ knows how it was all done. It must have taken a tortured mind. The difficulty is that, after Wylie had looked through all the CCTV footage, there's absolutely nothing obvious to see. Nothing, that is, until the precise moment of revelation. Apparently the security cameras are on what's called a continuous loop system. This is one that over-records after a period, wiping out the earlier recording period. Anyway the animal was clearly put there somehow. Obviously we need to find out how."

"Was the tape good, sir? Was it even working?"

"Well, DI Matilda."

Pawley looked back smiling gently.

"If you mean has DI Wylie started seeing things that are right under his nose these days, I think the answer may not be a definite yes. But actually in this case there were two pairs of eyes on the tape, his and mine, so I think it's pretty foolproof. In short, nothing conclusive was captured on the CCTV. We have an expert in that kind of stuff coming in to HQ soon to take a look at the tape in detail. Maybe there was some tampering. What we have to discover, and by we, I mean you two, is how on earth all of this was perpetrated in such a public place!"

Zac sat slightly straighter in his hard plastic chair.

"Sir"

"Yes lieutenant?"

"Something seems kind of freaky to me."

A smile played on George Pawley's lips. He was essentially kindly, and sarcasm not natural to him, so he merely raised a ragged eyebrow.

Zac continued.

"Well, we've got this ancient fortress-town of Windsor. It's a town with a medieval castle at its heart. It's the largest inhabited castle in the world, right?"

"Yes lieutenant?"

"Well the thing is, we know the whacko device used here is medieval. The weird thing for me is that this should've been done in such a flat out modern setting. I mean a shopping mall. It doesn't seem to stack up unless this nutcase is trying to make a point, if you see what I mean?"

Abbi nodded.

"I agree, sir. This thing has got everyone spooked. Why do it there? Why do it at all, something so grotesque?"

"Very well."

Pawley was clear in tone and manner.

"Let's get to the heart of this bizarre event. Go and talk to Wylie; see if he has made any other progress, and start looking into the background. I want to know if anything like this has happened before. Why Slough, and why that shopping centre and how did whoever it was evade the CCTV in doing it? Also look into where the swan was taken from. They are all tagged I believe as property of Her Majesty The Queen. It may be possible to identify the actual animal taken, though how this may help us I don't know."

"Sir?"

"Yes, DI Matilda?"

Abbi hesitated.

"Just to ask, sir… I was thinking… well… is all of this justified? I mean it's only an animal when all's said and done."

Pawley looked up with narrowed eyes.

"True. But this is no ordinary act, detective. This is sinister… and as you yourself said just now, bizarre. It isn't so much what kind of life was taken, but the manner in which it was done. This is what commands our attention. Also, and here I want to be understood most seriously, it is what it portends, what it might all mean from here on, that I fear."

The two young detectives made their return journey to Windsor Police Station with some grave questions on their minds.

Chapter Three

The next day Zac and Abbi were back on the antique streets of Windsor. The pretty garrison-town was standing smartly to attention at 12 noon, ready for inspection. They had gained nothing more from DI Wylie. It was clear to everyone that the videotape of the shopping centre would need proper technical analysis. They were taking a lunch break walking around Windsor. Zac was itching to look at other parts of the town. He wanted to know more about these modern-primitive people. To know why people went about their lives as they did. He wanted to know what the English did and if possible, why they thought it the only way to do it. Although he had little idea why some people do what they do, he was baffled by the rituals of these Windsor folk, so removed from his own Brooklyn world of drug deals, rub outs and drive-bys. What did these people bring forward from their bygone local past; from their families, embedded in the town like the cobblestones, going back centuries? How did they synthesise their past with the modern world? If there was one thing Zac had learned early on, it was that you don't challenge people's list of beliefs. These are the lists, he figured, that make us who we are. He put this to Abbi.

"Yesterday when I said Windsor's kind of like a private club, I meant that folk here have a real solid idea of what they believe in. A small town like this, real old and folk going real far back – when something happens like this weird stuff with the bird, I mean it can't be like, just random can it? There's gotta be like some background to it, right?"

"Is that a question or a statement Mr Dolby?"

Abbi hadn't been thinking of anything in particular at that second. She was in a mellow lunch-break mood.

"I guess both."

Abbi wrinkled her nose at him in a friendly smile. She liked this Yank. She teased him.

"You've stopped calling me ma'am."

Zac coloured.

"Yeah, well maybe I'm turning Limey."

"Don't lieutenant, we like you just the way you are."

Before Zac could register any pleasure at this, Abbi pointed to an above averagely high wall. "That's Victoria Barracks. Soldiering goes back a long way in this town."

"Sure seems like everything goes way back in this town, seeing as it's so damned old."

"Older than Disneyworld you mean?"

Abbi nudged him gently.

"Come on lieutenant, back to work!"

Zac smiled. He realised that in the end he hadn't developed his theory about the townsfolk or gained any insights about it from Abbi either. She had a charming and effective way of avoiding things she preferred not to discuss. They headed back to Windsor Police Station where they would be based for most of the time from then on unless summoned to Reading or elsewhere. The walk was ten minutes at the outside for two young people. Zac's cell rang. Abbi noticed he slipped deftly into a new mode. Walking parallel, he put a meter or two between himself and Abbi as he spoke.

"Yeah hi, Mom? Yeah it's wet. That's the deal over here Mom. No I didn't get the chance yet. Yeah Mom, of course I'm eating. What do you think, like I'm gonna starve myself? Yeah, yeah I'm wearing them… Mom, can we do this some other time?"

Abbi giggled quietly to herself as her new partner tried to extract himself from the maternal inquisition.

"All OK at home?"

Zac nodded his head over-vigorously.

"Oh heck yeah, it's all good. That was just my ahhh…"

"Your Mum?"

"Well, yeah my Mom."

The Police Station took pity on Zac by appearing before any further depiction of his doting Jewish mother was needed.

Back at the station Wylie was skulking around the coffee machines as Abbi lingered for a moment, waiting for Zac to visit the "bathroom" as Americans say. "You and the Yank come up with anything yet?"

"Have you?" asked Abbi simply.

"His name is Zac by the way."

"Slept with him yet?" Wylie smirked.

"Yes, of course! I mean he's been here all of seventy-six hours."

Wylie snorted looking beyond Abbi, then turned and walked off hurriedly.

"That hushed him up."

Zac was grinning.

Abbi blushed deeply. She'd been unaware that Zac was close behind her.

"Sorry. Wylie's still trying to cross the species barrier from reptile to homosapien, unsuccessfully as you can see."

"Sure sounds like a schmuck to me."

Abbi moved quickly on.

"Listen, I think you're really on to something with this medieval versus modern idea. I'm going to check-out some things online. Will you keep on top of the CCTV thing?

Zac responded.

"Sure. I wouldn't trust that guy Wylie to find his own navel in the bathtub. Anyhows there's something weird going on there for sure."

Abbi looked over.

"I mean, how come the bird just showed up out of nowhere? We need to check out what was covered by the

32

cameras. Are we meant to believe that one moment it's not there and the next it is?"

Abbi agreed.

"It's a good question. The tape's got to show up what went on."

She gently waggled her fingers at him in a slow goodbye.

"Better get going."

"Sure. Hook up later, Abbi?"

"Yes, let's."

Abbi smiled him a friendly smile as she headed off to her desk.

"This damned canteen specialises in stewing everything, especially the tea. What the….. .oh my God, Abbi! I didn't know you were here… and who is this attractive young man?"

"This is Lieutenant Zac Dolby from the New York Police Department. Zac, this is DI Amy Joss."

"It's an honour to meet you, ma'am."

"You too, detective."

DI Joss looked appreciatively at Abbi.

"You look good. How long have you been down here? What are you up to?"

"We're working on this… well… this thing in Slough. Have you heard?"

"Christ yes! What is all that about? It sounds like we've got a real nutter on our hands there."

"You part of this investigation, lieutenant?"

"Yes, ma'am, we're working on it right now."

Amy delved.

"So what brought you here in the first place Lieutenant Dolby?"

"Well I'm here on an exchange initiative to help solve inner-city crime, ma'am."

Amy Joss looked interested.

"But Windsor certainly isn't an inner city Mr Dolby."

"That's true, but they weren't quite ready for me in London, so I'm here for some weeks until they want me."

"I'm sure they'll want you once they've seen you."

33

Zac smiled.

"You from around here DI Joss?"

I certainly am, lieutenant. I live in Slough. I can show you around if you like?"

Abbi softly and slyly kicked the heel of the other woman's shoe.

"...Or not of course. Anyway, nice to meet you Lieutenant Zachery; see you again no doubt. You two had better go do some detecting. Let's catch up soon Abbi, I'll call you. Right now I've got the pile of paperwork from hell."

She smiled with meaning at Abbi and approvingly at Zac as she left.

Zac, politely:

"So long, DI Joss."

"Yes, bye Amy."

Abbi gave her a meaningful smile and an upward roll of the eyes. Turning back to Zac, she looked over at his notepad enquiringly.

"So what have you come up with?"

"Well, it looks like Wylie was right. There's absolutely nothing obvious to see on the CCTV. It's just the usual early morning stuff. The tape first picks up the mall guy at just after 7am making a pass of the mall. Shortly after he passes the mailman and they shout "hi" across the mall as they pass. There's no sound on the tape but it's kinda obvious. The mailman delivers the mail in a standard way to a number of stores. We need to talk to him urgently to find out if he saw anything."

Abbi cut him short.

"But wait Zac. Does the CCTV not pick up the scene of the swan and all the gore from the first moment?"

"No, it's just like Pawley said. There's like a moment when there's nothing, then next thing the whole scene's right there. It shows the mall manager standing with his back to the scene, talking on his cell."

"What time?"

"I'm pretty sure that's at 7.09, but I'll double check. Anyways the guy had his back to the camera. Then he like

34

moves out of shot, so the question is what did he see and when? Also how come no one else, including him, saw anything before it all just… showed up?"

Abbi cut in.

"One thing we do know from the security people is that this is a continuous loop tape that over-records itself every two and a half hours. So anything that may have happened earlier than the time when it starts to over-record won't be on tape. I'm arranging to meet with one of the security people later."

"OK, so the mall guy's gotta be pretty key to this, right? He discovered the dead bird. We need a second-by-second account of how he found it; maybe then we can figure out why nobody else saw it before him, and why he didn't find it until he did. Is he giving us some phony story, and if he is, why? I mean, it wasn't the kind of thing you could just miss!"

Abbi agreed.

"OK you get on to the postman. Maybe I can sit in on Wylie's interview with the centre manager. Brydson's his name if I recall correctly."

Zac grinned.

"Good luck with that!"

Abbi looked at her own notes.

"Oh yes and I've been looking into this Ripper thing. It is one of a whole ghoulish range of fifteenth century torture instruments. It was used against unfaithful women to tear away the breasts from the chest. To add to this, all through history the swan has been used as a symbol of female beauty. I'm not sure if this is what was meant here though. I'm going to try and find out why Slough was chosen, and any other pointers on the medieval front."

"OK sure."

Zac headed off smiling back at Abbi.

"Don't forget to gate-crash Wylie's interview!"

Chapter Four

Early that afternoon Zac picked his way towards Windsor general post-office via the backstreets. He purposely detoured past the looming castle walls and narrow streets holding apart the close-hugging old buildings. These leaned gently towards each other as if to prop each other up. They seemed to have grouped themselves into a secretive huddle, as if to ensure you didn't crack the mysteries of the ancient castle-town too easily. Zac spotted the colourful pink and black paintwork of the fascinatingly lopsided Market Cross House in the cobbled streets. Abbi's story ran that it leaned over at such a precarious angle because the Guildhall wanted more space and had pushed it out of the way. He walked on. By the time he got to Windsor Post-Office the queue was out of the door. This was because the last seven days on God's Earth had been a week of god-awful weather and all the elderly folk and the single mums had chosen this window of dry weather to get a few things done. He waited with a show of commendable patience and listened with half-closed eyes to the chatter in the queue and at the counter. At the bend in the crocodile nearest the counter he could hear some of the townsfolk being served.

"Yes, those forms used to be *blue* but now they're *pink.*"

"Oh yes, I remember that too, they *were* blue now you come to mention it."

Zac listened with interest to the townsfolk of this grey and curious island. A wide ribbon of blue nylon hanging between metallic posts guided the queue. It almost contained the post-office's clients, but bulged in parts where the town's very old or very young leaned on it, either oblivious or out of mischief. After some minutes he found himself at the head of the queue.

"Yes, hi ma'am, I'm looking for a Mr Duncan Dewer?"

The clerk looked friendly but baffled.

"I'm sorry sir; I don't know anyone of that name. Is he counter staff?"

"No, he's a mailman – a delivery guy."

The clerk looked clearer.

"Ok you want the back entrance, in that case sir. Just go out of here and turn left, then immediately left again. You'll come to the sorting office. Go in and ring the bell."

"Thanks for that, ma'am. It's a great help."

Zac followed the directions and within forty seconds was at the back of the post office, pressing a bell marked "Please Ring For Attention." After a moment or two, Mr Dewer identified himself from the back-room of the sorting office. He was part-bald and shaven-headed, wearing jeans slightly too young for him, trainers and a sweatshirt. He squeaked into that category of older men seeking younger women. He was cheerful and friendly.

"You're an American, right?"

"Yes sir, from Brooklyn New York. You know Brooklyn?"

"Me? No, never been to the US but I like baseball. We've got leagues over here now."

Zac got to the point.

"I understand you usually work out of Slough Mr Dewer?"

"Yes that's right, I only came in here today to see a mate of mine, Davey."

Zac looked up.

"As I say, he's a mate. He does a Windsor walk, so I meet him here sometimes."

Zac raised an eyebrow.

"A walk means a particular area or series of streets where you deliver the post for that day."

Zac understood.

"You know I want to ask you about this business in Slough?"

"Yeah, we were all really shocked. The idiots you get in the world today."

"Sure. Mr Dewer."

Zac looked down and through his notes.

"Can you tell me what you did on that particular morning, when the incident occurred, and if you saw anything that might shed light on these events?"

At this the postman became serious.

"Well, I can tell you what I did. I don't know if it will help you or not."

"Sure. Go ahead sir."

"Well I was on an early in Queensmere. I started there at 7am as always. I went round the shops and offices as normal. It was quite a light round actually. I saw Jimmy along the way."

"Jimmy?"

"Yeah, he's the centre manager. He's alright is Jimmy Brydson."

"Did you speak?"

"Not really, just shouted hello. I like to get the round over quick, then I have more time to myself, if you know what I mean? He just shouted over, hello there Dunc. That's short for Duncan, my first name."

"What time was that?"

"Just after 7am. I'd just started my round."

"You didn't see anything else then Mr Dewer- anything unusual?"

The postman looked back frankly but blankly.

"No, I didn't see anyone or anything except Jimmy. I just did my round as normal. Wish I could help, but it was just a normal day."

"What's a normal day, sir? It turned out, as you know, to be very far from normal."

The postman was straightforward.

"Well, security had probably been round as normal… then Jimmy did his rounds I guess, then me with my delivery. If Jimmy had seen anything by the time he passed me he'd have said something for sure. We've known each other since the beginning."

Zac raised an eyebrow again.

"The beginning?"

"Yeah, a bunch of us Scots came down here in the 1980's and got kind of drawn together, you know?"

"You mean guys who already knew each other from Scotland?"

"Well only some of us, the rest met down here. A big sorting office in Glasgow had just closed down and the good old Royal Mail put us on to opportunities down south. It was a huge office, so we didn't all know each other."

The postman's phrase *the good old Royal Mail* came across, Zac thought, as a little sarcastic. He continued his questioning.

"So you all ended up here, sir?"

"Not all, but yeah, a few of us. We met up in sorting and on delivery you know?"

"Anything else you can remember sir?"

Mr Dewer shook his head.

"Ok."

Zac was satisfied with this for now and wrote briefly in his notes.

"Right, thank you sir. We've looked over the videotape of the mall for that morning, and this all seems to tie up with your account. There are other unanswered questions of course, but we need to check out the tape further. From what we can see for the moment, as I say, you did what you say you did. We may need to talk to you again though. Thank you again, you've been very helpful."

"No probs, any time."

The Scotsman smiled an open friendly smile.

"You go to those baseball games yourself, right?"

Zac smiled back.

"Yeah I go to all the big games. You should come out to the States sometime."

The postman grinned in response.

"True. I'll have to save up though. This job doesn't pay much."

Zac felt satisfied with this first professional interchange with the people of this rain-sodden land. He checked his watch: time to hook up with Abbi. The thought pleased him.

Abbi indicated an upright chair with a smooth gesture of her small hand.

The security guard sat down.

"You are Mr Ken Steen?"

"Yes."

"Mr Steen, we're investigating a very nasty matter. I'm sure you're aware of it?"

"Yes miss, I couldn't believe it. I was there and yet I saw nothing."

"I understand this, and have read this remark in your statement sir, but sometimes we see things but we just don't realise that we have."

The security guard looked genuinely blank.

"Let me give you an example, Mr Steen."

Abbi quite enjoyed the raconteur part of her job. It made it feel like more of an art-form.

"Once, some time ago now, I lost a small bottle of Cava. Do you know what Cava is, Mr Steen?"

The man in front of her was not proud and seemed perfectly sincere.

"No, miss."

"Well, it's a Spanish version of Champagne. It can't be called Champagne though, because this would contravene trademark regulations. It looks the same though, and some would say tastes pretty much the same."

Mr Steen looked keen to help but baffled.

"Well it was a small bottle, and in order to keep it from my parents (I was only fifteen at the time), I thought it would be clever to take the label off the bottle, so that if it was discovered it might not be immediately obvious what it was. Stupid of course but I was only fifteen. Anyway I put it in a drawer with a number of other odds and ends. You follow me, Mr Steen?"

"Yes, miss. But I don't…"

"…Don't see what I mean, right?"

"Yes, miss. I mean, yes I don't."

"Ok, well here's what happened. I went to check on the bottle about a week later and found that it had gone. I was petrified that my mother had discovered the bottle, and was just biding her time to challenge me over it and cause a big scene. I looked everywhere in my room for the bottle just in case, ten times over, as you do, knowing all the time that I hadn't moved it. It'd just vanished."

The security guard tried to look as though he knew where this was heading.

"Right, well the next day I was still in a panic imagining all sorts of thing. So I decided to check my mother's kitchen cupboards. They were deep cupboards and I decided to take my torch, which I kept in same drawer as the one in which I'd hidden the bottle of Cava. Well, do you know what, sir?"

Mr Steen had to admit that he didn't in fact know what.

"When I picked up the torch… magically it'd turned into the small black-glass bottle of Cava."

The security guard looked as if possibly he had drawn the short straw in the female DI nutter competition, but was prepared to humour her.

Abbi continued with zeal.

"This was no conjuring trick, sir. This was merely me not seeing what was there; or if you prefer, me seeing what was there but choosing to ignore it. The torch I realised, had long gone, in exchange for some make-up I'd swapped with a school friend. But my brain insisted that each time I looked in the drawer, it was in fact a small black torch with a shape that tapered at one end, just like the small black glass bottle. The bottle had been there all along. Do you know what I am trying to tell you sir?"

41

The mild-looking muscular man in front of her said that he thought she meant that perhaps he could have seen something at the shopping mall which although he didn't realise it at the time, was significant to the terrible events of that day.

"Yes, Mr Steen, yes! And now that I've explained it all to you... was there anything!?"

"No miss, sorry. There was nothing."

Abbi looked at him like a disappointed child prodigy might look at a dim-witted adult who had acquired nothing new in the way of knowledge during his or her lifetime.

"Nothing, Mr Steen, are you absolutely sure about that? Think back. Is there nothing that occurs to you regarding that morning in Queensmere?"

The security guard looked as if he would like to have invented something to keep this attractive but impatient woman DI happy, but really couldn't help.

"There just isn't anything miss, I'm sorry."

Abbi realised that he was so genuinely sorry that she took pity on him.

"Ok here's my card, Mr Steen. If anything comes back to you, please call me OK?"

"Yes miss, of course."

"By the way, what time did you do your pass of the mall?"

"At 6am. It's recorded in my log if you would like to see?

Abbi looked at the screen of Mr Steen's electronic log.

"Thanks for that, sir. We may need to meet again."

Mr Steen slipped out apologetically as Zac came in.

"What did you get from the postman then?"

"Nothing. What did you get from the security guard?"

Snap. I think we need to get back online Mr Dolby."

"Drink first?"

"Yes, let's."

Zac looked down at his cell.

"Your mother again?"

"No, my aunt. I'll call her back later."

He returned his cell to his pocket quite tetchily Abbi thought.

Chapter Five

It was mid-morning of the next day and Zac and Abbi had taken to the streets of Windsor, squinting in a burst of late summer sun. Their first attempts at conversation were promptly interrupted by the sound of loud instrumental music, marching music, pomp, drumming and the barking of commands.

The marching military band and the tourist crowds were arranging the mid-morning ritual paralysis of the changing of the guard. Abbi pulled at Zac's sleeve in a friendly, un-police-like manner.

"Come on. Let's go up to the Guildhall Museum. I want to look up a few things that have been bugging me."

"Like…?"

"That instrument used to kill the swan. I think they may have some paraphernalia in there of a similar age. Let's go and see."

The traffic wardens and police support officers starting up their engines of self-importance. They would soon be out and about, holding walkie-talkies and sporting shiny badges. In their turn would come the undercover officers, dressed in an unvarying uniform of brown Brogues and tweed jackets, leading lovely velvety-eared Spaniels. Zac was again aware of an undertow of old secretive forces at work in the special and atypical town. He didn't know what they were, but he felt them all the same. Escaping the tourists and the band, they entered the grand interior of Windsor's Guildhall.

"I've made a loose appointment with a guy called Stuart."

Abbi dropped her voice now as the band had passed on and was curling up Castle Hill, towards the ancient gates of Windsor Castle itself.

A slightly comical figure in a corduroy jacket with wispy ginger hair waved at them.

"Stuart?"

"DI Matilda?"

"Yes, this is Lieutenant Zac Dolby."

"Morning sir, pleased to meet you."

The curator cocked his head on one side as if he had heard an odd noise.

"Now, you're an American aren't you? Are you here on secondment?"

"I am sir, NYPD."

"Really! Do you like it here lieutenant?"

"Well, it's OK so far sir."

The curator of the modestly-sized Guildhall Museum smiled.

"Ah, damned by faint praise lieutenant, faint praise!"

"No sir, really. I'm just getting used to things. You British have different customs, especially in an old town like this. Things go way back."

"Now there's an understatement, lieutenant! This museum is testament to that. Would you like to take a look around?"

Abbi nodded.

"We're interested in anything from the 15th century and particularly references to instruments of torture, or to the practice of it."

"Torture!?"

The curator seemed to the detectives almost unnervingly excited by this.

"Well, we have a couple of things in storage in the vault. We haven't brought them up yet. I can show you the references to them in the paperwork, which in turn is entered into the catalogue. We can also look at some of the folklore

45

that was typical in the town and the environs at the time if you wish?"

Abbi smiled encouragingly.

"That would be great sir, thank you."

The curator took down a large book with ragged binding from a shelf. "In terrible condition I'm afraid, but readable."

"Is this the catalogue you were talking about sir?"

"No lieutenant. I'll get round to that in a while. This is about folklore of broadly the 15th century in this part of the world. Look here. This is a reference from The Merry Wives of Windsor. Now that was later of course."

"Shakespeare?"

"Yes Miss Matilda, Shakespeare, but the tale was based on earlier local legend."

"This character referred to here."

He fingered a thick-cut page of yellowing paper.

"Is Herne the Hunter. This quote is from the Merry Wives, just here."

He caressed the thick paper fondly with a fat forefinger as he read:

Sometime a keeper here in Windsor Forest,
Doth all the winter-time, at still midnight,
Walk round about an oak, with great ragg'd horns.

"As the quote suggests, he was a keeper in Windsor Forest. The remains of this great wooded area is Windsor Great Park, not far from here lieutenant. You can still see some examples of what remains of the ancient oaks there, dating back hundreds of years, the forest itself thousands. They have over centuries formed themselves into some bizarre shapes. At night they can be quite frightening. I'm sure your colleague here will show you if you wish."

It seemed to the detectives that the curator had a sense of mischief about him.

"Anyway, eventually he was hanged from what came to be known as Herne's Oak, later cut down by Queen Victoria for firewood."

Abbi shifted a little impatiently.

"I think we need to look at the Catalogue of Artefacts."

"Yes of course, though the items I mentioned are not all recorded yet."

The curator closed the large ragged book and restored it to its shelf. Zac thought he seemed faintly irritated at being stopped in mid-flow, but covered his feelings over smoothly. He took out a much slimmer ledger from a drawer.

"This is my Entry Ledger. It shows all incoming items. These are eventually examined, dated and described. Finally they're entered into the Museum Catalogue proper. It will include any items dating from the 15th and 16th centuries. As I explained however they are not all recorded or on display as yet."

"Like this one?"

Abbi pointed to a numbered packing case marked on the page as "unopened".

"What is this?"

The curator's eyes gleamed fixedly on the page.

"Case number sixty-two. It hasn't been unpacked or catalogued yet, but I think it will be 15th century artefacts discovered in the depths of the castle in the 1930's. They lay forgotten in a corner somewhere and have remained untouched ever since, I believe. I'm itching to open the box but they have to be itemised at the time of opening and two people must be present."

"Shall we take a look now sir, there would be three of us?"

"Well that's very kind of you lieutenant, but it requires an official of the museum rather than an officer of the law."

He smiled a rather ghastly smile and moved on with the ledger.

"Here are some relics from the First World War.

"Thank you sir, we won't worry about those."

Abbi wasn't interested in the World War periods.

"Call us when you have opened that particular case, please sir."

She handed him a card. They left quickly, fearing another burst of enthusiasm from the curator might trap them in the Guildhall until closing time.

It was noon.

"Let's walk down that long path."

Zac pointed past tall ornate open gates.

Abbi smiled.

"The Long Walk you mean?"

Zac surveyed the dead-straight path trailing away in to the middle distance.

"Good name; yes, there."

"I want you to tell me as much as possible about the history of Windsor."

Abbi looked quizzical.

"Not sure I know much."

"OK, as an English person, just anything then that you know about Windsor – the royals for example."

Abbi thought.

"Well, the current line of succession, as you probably know, is the House of Windsor. The town of Windsor is considered the unofficial home of the current Queen, Elizabeth the Second and her family, who are descended from the Germanic House of Saxe Coburg-Gothe."

"So they weren't always called Windsor, right?"

"True, it was a cosmetic change. During the First World War, we were being gently annihilated by the Germans, and it sounded better to the British Public to call the royals something less Germanic, hence Windsor. This was the idea of the current Queen's father."

"Who's that?"

"George Five, Zac, as you Yanks like to say."

Abbi laughed as she spoke.

Zac went on.

"So the current outfit are all German?"

"Yes, all descended from Queen Victoria."

"That's the chick whose statue is outside Windsor Castle, right?"

"Yes, that's the chick!"

Abbi smiled to herself at what reaction this expression might stir in the townsfolk.

"So who got the job before Queen Tricky up there?"

"Well, if you want to know about before the Germans, you're talking about the House of Stuart."

"Scottish?"

"Yes, Scottish."

"So who ran the Scots out of town?"

"Well, it was a couple called William and Mary. He was Dutch by the way, William of Orange"

"Dutch, German, it all sounds kind of inbred."

"Yes, that's how Europe was. Maybe it still is a bit. It adds an intriguing dash of darkness to the old world, Mr Dolby!"

Zac grinned.

"Right, so this kind of A-list couple Bill Orange and his squeeze Mary get the job, what then?"

"Squeeze?!"

"Yeah."

Zac feigned unawareness of his comically casual terminology.

Abbi regained composure.

"The Act of Settlement."

"Huh?"

"Pay attention detective. The Act of Settlement 1701, which pretty much put us Protestants on the throne forever. The Scots were uncompromisingly Catholic, so when we took over it meant they'd reached the end of the line, if you'll excuse the pun."

"We?"

"Yes, I'm Royalist through and through. We're a true Protestant line, me and my folks. I'm a Royalist girl in a Royalist world…"

She hummed a bar or two of Madonna.

Zac mock-smiled.

"Yeah right. Don't call us, ma'am."

Abbi pretend-pouted.

"OK. But the Scots must have been pretty pissed, no? I mean they'd see it as being suckered out of the throne, right?"

"Right... and?"

"OK I get it, not mushy about losers?"

Abbi smiled radiantly back at him.

"Sorry, but no. They should've just tried a bit harder at the Battle of the Boyne. Anyway you Yanks need a bit of religious balance over on your side of the Pond too, right? I mean to balance out all those Latin Catholic types?"

Zac laughed.

"What would I know, I'm Jewish!"

"Special you mean?"

"Why, don't you believe in the Special Relationship, Miss Matilda? You old Brits and us young upstart Yanks?"

Abbi pushed him gently off the narrow ribbon of tarmac of the Long Walk onto the grass. Zac pushed her gently back. It was a moment of closeness.

"Old! Cheek!"

"I merely mean, Miss Matilda, that you Brits go real far back right?"

"We go farther back than you Yanks, it's true."

Zac was pretty comfortable with his English oppo, but still intrigued by things that he had never encountered back in the clamour of New York. In fact, subjects and matters that seemed utterly removed from his life and that of everyone he knew. He felt the old world drawing him in. Echoes of ancient doings and deeds were overtaking the fresh-faced foreigner with invisible, addictive fumes.

"So Abbi, go further back into the past. What started all this England-is-so-special thing, and created a power that conquered half the world?"

Abbi thought seriously for a moment.

"Maybe if I tell you about the Magna Carta, very briefly, she emphasised, that'll shut you up?"

"May do."

She looked at him play-menacingly.

"Right. The Magna Carta was or is a sort of mission statement put together by a bunch of nobles, pissed off with the then King – John – who was in the habit of making up the law as he went along. It was signed in 1215, at Runnymede, about six minutes from where we're standing as the crow flies."

"And how did it change things?"

"It made sure everyone, including royalty, was accountable to the law of the land. Even you Yanks came out with your own Magna Carta for Dummies a few hundred years later, which you call the Declaration of Independence, I believe. "

Zac smiled.

"Right, so like everything else, you Brits did it first?"

Abbi fixed him with another alluring grin.

"And better of course. The Declaration of Independence is really just the big print version of the Magna Carta with the difficult bits taken out."

Zac didn't mind playing the young upstart to Abbi's mother-country teasing. She was easily pretty enough to carry it off.

"Ok, so what happened post-Magna Carta?"

"Well, as you'd expect from a megalomaniac man of the time, or any time come to that, he went back on his promise. The Pope allowed him to scrap the whole thing. He died a year later however, and somehow it was reinstated and became a permanent fixture. It became in time, the foundation of the world famous British Judicial System."

Zac looked impressed as Abbi paused.

"OK, so even though this King John guy was a bit of a schmuck, the Crown remained popular and this town is pretty much devoted to keeping up the good name of the monarchy and the image of the British Royal Family?"

"That's true!"

They walked on. Here and there, lovers walked together in pairs of kindred feeling. Birds and jets flew higher and farther off overhead. It could have been any town in England except for the unanswerable fact that it was Windsor; a special town and a special case.

Abbi pointed.

"The flag flying at full-mast means The Queen is in residence."

Zac thought he should say something in response.

"Good egg."

Abbi laughed.

"Good egg?"

"Well, isn't she?"

"Yes, yes."

Abbi was sure in her tone.

"She is."

They paused looking back at Windsor Castle from the advanced point they had reached on the Long Walk. Abbi gave in to her natural curiosity.

"Your life over there -"

"Aha?"

"What was it like, lieutenant? Was it better than here?"

Zac smiled.

"You wanna know, right?"

"Well, maybe. Yes."

"Ok. So like I told you I was just getting along with my life. The NYPD is just buzzing. Life on the streets is tough; shake downs, scams, The Mob. That's the Sicilian connection, if you get me?"

"The Mafia?"

"Yes, them."

Abbi grinned.

"Do they really carry violin cases with machine guns inside?"

"That's more the old days, gangsters like Al Capone, detective. But it's been known."

They laughed at the absurdity of the image in a modern policing world.

They looked intently at each other in silence for a very long five or six seconds. The spell was broken by Abbi's mobile.

"Yes, Wylie?"

She didn't sound friendly... silence for twenty seconds.

"What? Who is it? When did this happen?"

Abbi shivered visibly, dropping her mobile back into her bag.

"This is bad, lieutenant, very bad."

Back at the station Abbi was business-like. She addressed Wylie.

"Who're we seeing first?"

"Whoever you two decide upon... together. They'll be expecting you in Eton as soon as. Some bloke with a fancy degree is looking at the body."

He sounded sulky.

"My big job is to get the forensics report sorted, so hurry Einstein up if you can, will you?"

"Thanks for bringing us up to speed, Wylie. We do need forensics in detection work you realise? Some jobs require more than just getting hunches."

Abbi looked over at Zac with a ghost of a smile on her face.

Wylie paused, assessing whether or not to rise to the bait.

"The dead man was identified around 11am today. His colleagues got worried when he didn't turn up for work."

"Who is he? What did he do?"

"Steady on there, lieutenant"

Wylie seemed irked by the rapid questioning.

"One thing at a time."

He turned back to Abbi.

"This guy was done in by another of those weird old-fangled gadgets. He was forced into a pair of old stocks that have been lying outside some restaurant over the bridge in Eton for the last god knows how many years. Whoever is behind this is a nutcase, I'm telling you."

"When was this?"

Wylie condescended to reply to the American this time.

"He was first discovered this morning early, 8am I think, but not identified until he was missed, which as I said, was at around 11am. Forensics will let me know exact time of death when they know. Anyway children, I'll see you when you get back, I've got to prepare for my Jimmy Brydson interview tomorrow."

Chapter Six

Eton was quiet when they arrived. Again they came upon 'Police Do Not Cross' tape. It billowed out in the windy early afternoon. The sun had made way for showers, which were dodged by locals without drama. They approached the scene, one on the heels of the other. Abbi led the way with a friendly nod at the SOCO's.

Abbi spoke first.

"Here we go again lieutenant."

Zac looked about him. The police cordon was more sparsely manned than in Slough.

"This is Eton, right?"

"Yes sir."

This was supplied by a uniformed officer with a respectful nod to Zac.

"So what's happened here constable?"

"Timothy McManus, miss, a housemaster at Eton College found dead in the old stocks that stand outside the Cockpit Restaurant. He was discovered with a... well a turnip in his mouth, but actually he was suffocated by clear plastic bag tied tightly at the neck. Shall we go to the scene miss?"

They walked the twenty yards or so to where the body was covered over by a small white forensics tent. The old stocks lay to one side of the tent, covered separately.

Zac leaned over for a closer look, gesturing to a few items scattered around.

"They must've taken those chains off that were anchoring these bad boys to the wall with a hacksaw or something like that. It must've taken some strength to do that. Ditto force the guy into this gizmo."

Abbi was addressing the man inside the tent.

"DI Matilda and Lieutenant Zac Dolby, Thames Valley."

The police pathologist half turned looking unimpressed.

"What do you want to know detectives, and don't say time of death. I told some prat colleague of yours, tomorrow morning at the earliest."

Zac and Abbi exchanged glances.

"That would be DI Wylie, sorry about him. The lieutenant and I hope to be a little more, let's say, subtle in our approach."

"Sorry, yes of course. John Courtenay police pathologist, pleased to meet you. That Wylie character really got on my nerves."

"We do appreciate your tolerance. About this death though, can you tell us what happened to this guy?"

"Well lieutenant, he had a nasty time of things I can certainly tell you that. He was put into those old stocks before death. A turnip was forced into his mouth as some kind of humiliation I guess. Then a clear plastic was bag placed over his head. As I say, I need to get the body back to the lab for proper post-mortem, but from the colour of the face I would say as a first guess, he was suffocated slowly and painfully. It would have taken a few minutes to be fatal, but through the clear plastic the killer would have been able to see the life draining slowly out of him. Very nasty indeed."

Abbi's eyes searched methodically up and down the corpse.

"Will there be any forensics on the body from the killer, do you think?"

"I really can't say until I have any potential samples taken and tested. I'll let you know as soon as. Maybe I can have your card DI Matilda?"

Abbi passed it on. They exited the forensics tent.

Abbi tutted.

"The problem is there is absolutely no CCTV in Eton at all."

"I suppose it would spoil the character?"

Abbi smiled at him.

"That, Lieutenant Dolby, is the perspective of an overseas visitor to a quaint historic town. Eton is actually a working town, not a museum piece. At some point soon we'll need to see the housemaster's wife and his Eton School House. The boys' in his charge will be pretty upset by this."

John Courtenay poked his head out of the forensics tent as they were starting to head off.

"Oh, I forgot this."

Abbi took a small white card from his hand. It was identical in size and type to that found under the dead bird in Slough.

"What does it say Abbi?"

She held out the white card for Zac to read:

Virecit Vulnere Virtus.

"How's your Latin, Mr Dolby?"

Zac looked sheepish.

"That's more a matter for you old-country guys isn't it?"

"This is England you do realise, not ancient Rome? Either way we'll get onto it back at Windsor Nick."

It was 8pm. Abbi sat smilingly facing Zac amidst the good people of the castle-town's best curry-house.

"Isn't Slough better for curry?"

Zac looked shyly and appreciatively at the after-hours Abbi. Curves and curls were all in evidence and in the right balance.

"It is really but this is a good way to get a feel for Windsor-folk in their natural habitat."

Abbi too had an eye for Zac's non-detective qualities. In the curry-house everything was in order. Everything and everyone was in the right place. Nobody was quite on the same footing as the indigenous townsfolk; not quite part of the local chain of being.

Fingers were clicked at a waiter.

"Excuse me, more *Roald* please!"

The waiter was confused.

"Sir?"

"Roald, Roald, you know *dhal,* Roald Dhal*!*"

The table of middle aged professionals sniggered and the waiter also laughed obligingly. Deaf to the noise, Abbi was keen to lock detective minds on the macabre events that had cast such a shadow over the Royal Borough in the last few days.

"Let's go over what we've got."

They spoke and ate, now fascinated by the subject and each other's company. Abbi resumed.

"So in Slough we get the ritual killing of a mute swan, a powerful symbol of The Queen's presence in the whole area but in this town especially. So why Slough and not Windsor? We know that the slaying was of a poor defenceless animal. Additionally it is well recorded that the swan is a motif often employed to betoken a woman's beauty, especially a swan's neck. The instrument used in this ghastly act is a 15th century torture instrument, and was used against women deemed to have been unfaithful. There's also an illustration of a swan and her cygnets, yet to be assessed properly. Now today, we have just encountered another example of medieval torture, this time used against a man. Wylie is supposed to be looking into any forensics on that. So things are wildly more serious. This is now a case of a human murder. The media, Amy tells me, are already crawling all over it, so tomorrow may be fun if you get my drift?"

Abbi paused and looked ahead of herself, as if still trying to drink in the full significance of the situation.

Zac filled in some blanks.

"OK so here's where we're at with the mailman and the video. We've got jack on the tape up to now. There's gotta be some shenanigans on how the swan got to the shopping mall but didn't show up on the looped-tape. We're getting a frame by frame lowdown on that from some geek right? We know from the pathologist John Courtenay that there's currently no forensics at the scene. Also we know there's some weird symbolism going on with these medieval gizmos. Ditto the other bunch of stuff you mentioned Abbi. Then there's the Eton Housemaster guy, killed real nasty in this medieval theme. Next we get this spiel on a white card found on the body of Mr MacManus. According to Amy it translates as something like *courage is greater through adversity*. She did Latin at school. We don't know how it ties up with the hit though. We do know that nobody saw anything in Eton, or at least this is what we assume unless someone comes forward or we pick someone up. Like I say, we're still waiting for forensics on that one... Abbi?"

Abbi started as though wakened from a dream. She sounded both excited and, Zac thought, a little scared.

"Listen Zac, this is all beginning to remind me of something."

Zac stared back expectantly.

"Well, actually I'm sorry but I can't tell you."

They fell in to an awkward silence for a minute. The first since they had first met.

Abbi got up.

"I'm going back to the hotel."

"But you haven't finished up."

"Yes I know. I really am sorry Zac. See you tomorrow."

Zac intervened while he could.

"Yeah sure, but don't forget we're moving into police quarters from tomorrow morning first thing?"

Abbi made for the door.

"Yes, we'll be neighbours I suppose. Bye."

The American was left sitting in the restaurant puzzled and a little angry.

They had parted on a strained note. He felt slightly more distant at that moment from the very English town and the British people. He felt his first pang of homesickness for Brooklyn.

Chapter Seven

Zac stepped out onto the shadowy singular streets of Windsor as the day faded out. According to the flag, The Royal, the head of state and figurehead of an old and once great empire, was still in residence. Zac reckoned that all the usual traits of human nature were reflected in and by this small and special town. Equally he reasoned, undeniably special though Windsor certainly was, scratch the surface and it was pretty much like any town and every town anywhere. What he had to find out was what was behind these creepy events. Like the town of Slough up the road, the same forces of human nature had got to be at work. He walked on for a while along the river in silent thought. The evening was beautiful and contrasted with his gloomy reflections. He took to the role of detective-observer. The medieval folk that had caroused in the streets were still here. The same people simply divided by interval of a few hundred years, but surely the same people. They had the same faces, the same genes. Only the names had changed. The same townsfolk were here, sitting outside the all-day alehouses from early morning, swearing, spitting and cackling. Still here were the men, shouting lewd remarks to their women-folk, also cackling with coarse laughter. The outsider in Zac looked on shrewdly at the doings of the people of the regal, turreted town. It was modern life in an ancient setting, wedded to the past by umpteen generations of its people. Habits and traditions had been handed down, family to family. Zac's presence in Windsor he realised, was simply the blink of an eye. The backdrop hadn't changed, only the costumes and the names above the shops. The main stage-set hadn't changed either. The castle still ruled supreme. He returned to his hotel, but didn't go straight to his room. Instead he sat in a deep armchair in the hotel lounge with his laptop. He wanted to know what drove the people on this island of bedevilled weather and its age-old rituals. He particularly wanted to know why he felt so shut out from English minds and their past of long-guarded secrets. Even his female DI oppo was going secretive and weird on him. He didn't like it.

Zac was jolted upright by loud knocking at his hotel bedroom door.

Damn, its moving into digs day he thought; it must be his lift and he wasn't even dressed.

"Hang on… sorry… just a second."

"Can I come in? Are you decent?"

Zac's mind changed gear.

"Oh sure, yes… of course, please do."

"You *are* decent, shame!"

Abbi smiled a cheeky and apologetic smile in his direction.

"Guess who's outside?"

Zac looked quizzical.

"The papar*rats*!"

"The press?"

"Yes, well that's the polite term. I did say they would be."

"So what's the deal, Miss Matilda?"

Abbi looked back at him wide-eyed and cocky.

"The deal? You're a grown up police-person too detective."

"Yes, but this country is alien to me ma'am."

Abbi laughed out loud.

"You are the alien hereabouts lieutenant. Ok stand behind me. Now what we do is we go out and get in to that white van, OK?"

"What white van?"

Abbi pointed out of the window. Her movements and excitement conjured up a small vortex of activity in the room.

"Look, it's supposed to be taking us to Ward Royal. We have facing apartments, it's exactly one minute. Get your cases."

Zac looked star-struck in the limelight of Abbi's flashing green eyes. She roused him in to life.

"Come on Zac! Let's hope that van can shift. If they know where we're going to live we'll never get a moment's peace."

She led the way out of the hotel.

The white van ran a red light and lost the last of the journalists to make it in a short burst of speed to the bleak-looking grey housing complex, where they would be neighbours.

"Ward Royal sir, miss."

"Thanks Steve."

They wheeled their respective suitcases towards facing doors on the narrow concrete aisle between apartments and let themselves in.

"Meet here in thirty?"

"Yes lieutenant. Do you feel safe now, or do you want me to come and tuck you in?"

Zac laughed and closed the door.

Abbi approached Wylie at his desk.

"So when're you seeing him?"

No response.

"Listen Jamie, I just want to sit in. It's not a judgment on you."

Wylie looked mistrustful.

"Oh, it's Jamie now is it?"

"Well we were once on very friendly terms right?"

"Yes, DI Matilda, but times change."

"Yes, but we're all on the same side right?"

"You're on the Yank's side more like."

Abbi was angry.

"You're jealous aren't you? That's what this is all about isn't it?"

Wylie snorted, not answering the question.

"You can always go over my head. Go to George Pawley."

"I don't want to do that!"

"You'll have to."

"Great, not at all childish then?"

Wylie walked up the corridor and out of view.

"No joy then?"

Zac came up softly making Abbi jump.

"You'd make a bloody good assassin detective. Don't sneak up!"

"So Wylie won't play ball?"

"No, he's an idiot, but I've got an idea."

"Amy listen, I need to get that weasel Wylie to let me in on the Brydson interview. What lever can we use? It needs at least two detectives present otherwise Wylie is bound to miss something vital. Is there any way we can apply pressure?"

Amy Joss concentrated hard. Abbi waited.

"Yes, OK I'll remind him about the Johnson case – that should do it."

"What was the Johnson case?"

"Wylie was sole interviewer in the case of a guy called Sammy Johnson. He missed out some vital questions at interview. The next day the guy was found shot dead."

"God, really? Won't it be a bit delicate, especially if he knows you told me?"

"Not really Abbi. I was seeing Wylie myself until I found out what a creep he was. So you could say I've got the power!"

Amy Joss gave her a joyously wicked look. She then looked Abbi up and down.

"You look happy."

Abbi grinned in return.

"Is there a law against it DI Joss?"

"There probably should be! Are you seeing him?"

"That my dear, is none of yours!"

"Isn't it against the rules Abbi?"

"Ha, rules! He's only here on secondment. He isn't employed by Thames Valley. I'd say that makes him fair game!"

Abbi grinned and headed out of the room.

"Oh, and thanks for the favour on this Amy."

She went off to look for Zac.

Zac was impressed.

"Really, did that actually happen? OK when is the interview then?"

"I'm checking that out with front desk."

"You're one scary lady ma'am."

"Thanks lieutenant. I'll take that as a compliment."

Abbi looked down at her mobile.

"Yes?"

Silence…

"Yes sir, I *would* like to know."

Silence for perhaps thirty seconds

"So nothing in the way of medieval items then?"

Silence…

"Ok, I may be back in touch."

Zac looked enquiringly.

"The museum guy right?"

"Yes, says there's nothing interesting in the boxes."

"That's a damn shame!"

Abbi reflected.

"It doesn't change anything major for us does it?"

Zac disagreed.

"It means that things of interest may have been lifted from the trunk. If they were they could still be used against someone else. Who knows how many more of those gross gizmos may be out there?"

"Yes I suppose so. I did want to see other examples like the device that was used on the swan."

"Let's see what we can get out of this mall guy. Even if Wylie goes ape, we gotta move on."

Abbi nodded. The case was slowing up and she was not one to let the grass grow.

In the end, Wylie was sulkily OK about Abbi's attendance at the centre manager's interview.

"I am informed that's good practice for two of us to do this. It helps eliminate possible errors of er... interpretation, shall we say."

"Yes, that's right DI Wylie. I'm glad you don't mind."

"I don't mind at all DI Matilda. As you know I always play by the rules."

"Yes, especially when you're forced to."

Abbi smiled at him playfully.

The door clicked open and the Queensmere Centre Manager, James (Jimmy) Brydson, was shown in to the interview room. There was no implication that he was being interviewed under caution, and he seemed relaxed and friendly.

"I'm DI Wylie. Thanks for coming in, Mr Brydson."

"That's OK sir, I want to help. This whole thing has been upsetting for me and the whole family. I'd like to put it all behind me."

"This is DI Matilda. She'll be present during the interview."

Mr Brydson smiled in Abbi's direction.

"I may have a question or two to ask myself, Mr Brydson."

Wylie looked faintly displeased at this comment but said nothing to Abbi.

"Mr Brydson, can you just start by confirming your job at Queensmere Shopping Centre in Slough?"

The centre manager looked across frankly at the detectives and moved to make himself more comfortable in the standard issue plastic chair. He gave the impression that he was prepared to talk fully and frankly.

"Yes of course. I'm the Centre Manager at Queensmere in Slough. My job starts very early in the morning and finishes quite often late at night. Queensmere isn't a big shopping facility by comparison with say Bluewater or Arndale, but it still involves a great deal of time and coordination."

"Go on."

Wylie added to Abbi's encouragement.

"Yes, Mr Brydson, please go on. What does your day-to-day work involve?"

"Well, that's a question!"

The centre manager smiled back. To the detectives, on the face of things he was likable and easy-going.

"Well, Mr Brydson?"

Brydson was keen to explain.

"As I say, I start very early and oversee almost all activities."

"Give us some examples Mr Brydson?"

Abbi looked over at Wylie and mouthed a silent sorry that she didn't mean.

Brydson continued.

"I'm involved with things like purchasing. For example I will deal with the buying in of products such as lighting or paving. I also deal with any business opportunities that come up. I mean, say a large retail chain wants to set up in the centre. I'd be involved in all the negotiations from start to finish. It doesn't mean that I do all of it on my own of course, but I'm present for most of the meetings. I know which shops are in the centre at any one time, and the shops that are soon to open or close. Plus I know most of the people involved. I also deal with budgeting and I oversee hiring of centre staff. I don't mean the staff of the individual shops mind, just those people running the centre itself."

"Do you choose the centre staff Mr Brydson?"

Detective Wylie kept a steady eye on the other man.

"We have a global recruitment function for the group which is operated centrally, but I can veto a choice of a staff member if I feel strongly enough."

Abbi looked across keenly.

"Have you had to veto anyone recently?"

"No, nobody miss."

"What kind of qualities do you need in your job, would you say?"

Brydson looked half amused at Wylie's question.

"Am I being interviewed for my own job, detective?"

Wylie smiled dryly back at him.

"No, it's just to know what sort of day-to-day interaction goes on; it may help us understand what happened."

"Sure, well you have to be everyone's friend, a team player as the expression goes, yet at the same time the one to show leadership. Oh yes, and you have to be bloody well organized."

"More than in any other job?"

Abbi's question drew a lively reaction from the centre manager.

"Well miss, if a van-load of dangerous chemicals turns up in the wrong service road and collides with a fruit and veg lorry, and untrained staff try to sort out the mess, I can be in trouble on about ten separate legal counts!"

Wylie and Abbi looked as though they both understood this point.

Wylie looked down at his notes.

"OK Mr Brydson, moving on to the morning in question. Please can you just run through your day. I know it may not sound important, but please just start from getting up that day, and run through up to the point when you discovered the …er scene."

"OK."

Abbi looked up from her own notes

"Oh, yes, and if you can please add in timings where you know them."

"I got up on that day at 4am, same as always. My wife works normal hours so I have to sneak about."

"What does she do?"

"She's in the prison service miss."

Abbi nodded.

"I get out of the house about 4.45am."

"So it takes you quite a while to get ready?"

"Yes sir, I have to make the wee ones' lunch and have some breakfast myself."

"How many children do you have Mr Brydson?"

"Just the two. A boy and a girl. A gentleman's family as they say".

Abbi smiled and signalled with her eyes for him to go on with his story.

"I'm at my desk by 5am of a morning. It's a mile from home, so I'm well placed if I'm needed in a hurry, which I often am."

"Do you drive in Mr Brydson?"

"No sir, I cycle."

Wylie was surprised.

"All weathers?"

"Yes, I find it helps my management of the centre."

Both detectives looked puzzled.

"Well the thing is if you drive a car, you park it in the car park in full view of everyone. That way all the staff and anyone else know where you are. They know that you are in and on the prowl so to speak."

Wylie still looked mystified, but Abbi seemed to have got it.

"Well detective as you know, when the cat is away…What I mean is, by cycling in I can put my bike in any number of little cubby-holes and the staff don't know if I'm at work or not. This means they're always on their toes; better productivity, better attitude."

Wylie tried to give the impression he'd understood this point from the start by simply moving on without comment.

"Thanks Mr Brydson. So you're at work. What now?"

"So, I get to my desk at 5.00am as I said. I generally have a very quick coffee to get me started so to speak, and set off to do my early pass of the centre, taking in the main avenues of the mall between about 5.15am and 5.30am. This gives me time to stop and see if things are secure and functioning as they should be."

"What would that include sir?"

"I make sure all the shop fronts are secure. Sometimes I try the doors if I suspect there could've been an attempted entry."

"And on the day in question?"

"Nothing untoward, miss. I went from the north end to the south, then out of the mall on to Slough High Street."

"Is the High Street part of your official pass-through?"

"Not exactly sir, but I like to see if there are any well, undesirables about."

Wylie seemed more than satisfied with this answer. He liked his job as a DI, and Abbi knew even without looking over at him, the zealous look he'd be wearing when it came to discussing *undesirables*. Wylie had his eyes fixed firmly on the man in front of them.

"What then?"

Mr Brydson shifted in his seat.

"I went back to my office and caught up with paperwork until 7am. Then I did my second pass of the mall."

Abbi's pen hovered over her notes.

"So Ken Steen the security guard, did you see him?"

"No, he passes through at 6am, but if there's nothing to report I don't see him. I get his electronic log later on in the day."

"Did you do the exact same walk through as earlier, Mr Brydson?"

Brydson looked Abbi thought, very faintly defensive at this.

"Pretty much, miss."

"So you have walked from the north to the south end again?"

"Yes, and then as always on to the High Street and scanned the mall side of the street as far as possible. Then I went back in to the mall to do the return walk-through."

Abbi listened intently.

"Did you go back exactly as you had come?"

"Almost."

"Almost?"

"Yes, well I usually look in on my bike on the second pass, on the way back to my office. There's an alcove to the right-hand side of the mall. As I check the shop doors on the opposite side, I just put my head round into the alcove to check on it as I go."

"But not the first time round?"

"No, I would only just have left it there on the first run."

Wylie asserted himself.

"So, both at this stage, 7.am Mr Brydson, and then just after 7.am when you greet the postman Duncan Dewer, you're unaware of the crime-scene?"

"Totally, *totally* unaware; there was nothing that could have prepared me for that!"

The centre manager looked pale and genuinely upset at recalling the scene, and both the detectives paused momentarily for him to recover his composure.

"Ok Mr Brydson. We realise that you are suffering a fair bit because of all of this, but we really need to get to the bottom of what you saw, and hopefully what happened."

Abbi's gentle female tone seemed to calm Brydson. He did continue to exhibit a tremor in his voice though, as he came to the hard facts.

"Like I said, I walked back up on the right-hand side of the mall, about as far as the joke shop."

The detectives stayed very still, still and silent, as if the man was a deer they were stalking and needed not to startle. Clearly he was nervous as he continued.

"As I said before, at just after 7am I passed Dunc, Mr Dewer that is, just to say hello do/if you understand?"

Abbi kept her commentary to a minimum.

"OK."

"It was at the point where the glass atrium reaches its peak, so about halfway down the mall. Then, about a minute or so later, I had a phone call and stopped to answer it. At that point I had my back to the… well... you know what…"

"Who was the call from sir?"

"My wife miss. Nothing important, just practical stuff about the kids' tea you know?"

Abbi nodded.

"So I answered the call, though I'm not really too happy talking when I'm at work. I don't like to be distracted. I see myself as a bit of a perfectionist if you follow me?"

Wylie asked.

"So you kept it short?"

"Yes sir, I was as quick as possible."

Abbi again:

"What direction were you facing at this point, Mr Brydson?"

"I was facing to the north end when I was first on the phone. I had my back to the scene."

"You had your back to the northward facing camera which is located at the southern end of the centre?"

"Yes sir. That's it."

"So you hadn't completely turned round at that point?"

"No, I was just turning as I hung up miss. It was at that moment that I caught sight of a red blur out of the corner of my eye."

"Red blur?"

Wylie wanted more detail.

"Yes, it was just a strong primary colour hitting me in the face. I couldn't understand at first what I was actually looking at. It was a bit like when you open the curtains after a heavy snow fall, you know? I mean you're not quite ready for the sudden difference in the scene you're looking at."

The two detectives seemed to get this quite easily. Wylie pushed on.

"So, you looked and you saw what?"

"As I said it took me a minute to sum it up. I saw the blood, I saw the white of the bird, and I saw the wet blood shining on the paving slabs. It seemed like a butcher had set up shop in the open."

Abbi was keen to define things in more detail.

"How was it that you hadn't seen any of this on the way down? Are you saying that it wasn't there, or that you were so focused on your trawl of the shops on the right-hand side, you may have missed it?"

"Missed it?"

The centre manger sounded incredulous.

"How could I have missed it? It wasn't there before, simple as that!"

He looked quite angry at the suggestion.

Abbi retracted.

"I'm sorry Mr Brydson, it's just that I… we, need to go through it all with a fine toothcomb. You'll have to forgive me if I didn't understand your account at first."

Abbi's police training paid off.

Brydson looked down as he spoke.

"It's OK miss, I'm sorry. It's just that it was so horrific. No one could have missed it. It sort of spread across the whole mall in a way, even though it wasn't across it all, if you see what I mean?"

"Not really."

Jamie Wylie was not a man to make subtle or abstract interpretations.

Brydson looked up again more sharply.

"I mean that even though it didn't cover the whole area, because the blood was shining and the light was quite bright through the atrium glass, it sort of projected further."

Abbi saw exactly what he meant.

"We understand totally Mr Bryson, it must have been awful."

Wylie looked sulky at this intervention but let it pass. Taking charge again:

"So, what did you do sir?"

"I didn't know what to do."

The centre manager looked down again, deflated.

"I felt completely helpless."

Wylie's movements gave away his impatience.

"OK, but what in fact did happen next sir?"

Chapter Eight

In Eton Zac made his way to the address given for the deceased housemaster, Timothy MacManus. To Zac, Eton looked like the quintessential old-world small town setting. He understood from those in the know that it was nonetheless very much a working town. He sized up the world renowned public school as he passed. It was, Pawley said, the maker of many British Prime Ministers and great men of state. To Zac it was a fascinating window into the past. Things existed here which had died out nearly everywhere else, solely because they are in the service of the famous public school. The rows of quaint shops running along both sides of the High Street from Eton Bridge nearly as far as the College vied for his attention. These were shops frozen in time. He passed Thomas's, the Eton Boys' Barber and the "Tailor and Hosier since 1784." He realised that his own professional dealings now straddled not only the mellow-bricked old-world privilege of this select Eton Boys' School, but also the gritty and sinister dealings in Slough, just five minutes away up the hill. If at all, how did these two very different places connect? Timothy MacManus had been a housemaster to a clutch of promising sixteen year old – year 12 – boys. Zac knew very little about the education system in England or how it matched up with his own Bronx County High School in New York. He could tell even now though, walking up the ancient High Street that the two places differed a great deal. They were like different worlds and Zac was the outsider, an alien. Not that Eton was typical of England either, it was not. Eton was also special. The door to the master's house was answered by Mrs MacManus herself. Zac thought immediately she was a woman of character. Here she was having just lost her husband, but still here she was, taking charge and getting on with things. How very British Zac thought. How very old-school.

"You are the detective?"

"Yes ma'am, yes I am. Lieutenant Dolby, ma'am, Zac Dolby."

"Please come in detective. Come in to the library and take a seat."

"Thank you so much ma'am."

Zac positioned himself a little uncertainly on what looked to his unschooled New York eyes like an unnaturally elongated chair.

"Please sit in the wing-chair Mr Dolby, the chaise-longue is really frightfully unforgiving on the back. I have no idea why we keep it."

"Ma'am, can I just say how sorry I am for your loss."

Mrs MacManus looked over at the American with a motherly eye. Let me get you some tea and cake lieutenant."

Zac nodded obligingly. He didn't want to offend, and actually kind of liked the idea of this very English ritual.

"That would be swell ma'am, thank you."

The order for tea and cake went out to a functionary and Zac looked over sheepishly at a world he knew nothing about.

"Ma'am your husband, do you know... well... why this could have happened?"

Mrs MacManus looked over at the young foreigner.

"Have you been here in England long Mr Dolby?"

Zac pondered this question. He wanted to get on with the facts but clearly this was a woman of distinct methods and protocol. If the game was to be played at all it would be done on her terms.

"No ma'am, I really haven't. I wasn't looking to move overseas, but it just sort of happened."

Mrs MacManus smiled.

"I think someone had a plan for you detective. It's possible that this adventure will be the making of you. Never underestimate the power of fate."

She looked down for a long second.

"He was a wonderful man you see."

Zac kept silent.

"He meant everything to me and to the boys of course. He was a guiding light. I cannot believe he's really gone. None of us can."

Zac found this aspect of the work hard. He faltered for a second before going on.

"I know I can't truly understand, Mrs McManus, and I am sorry for this, but please bear with me while I go through the questions I have, and then I will be straight out of your way."

She smiled mutely for him to proceed.

"Well the thing is I've spoken to SOCO, scene of crime officers that is, and also to the police pathologist who... well... who examined your husband. The feeling is ma'am, that that this was some kind of ritual attack. Have you any thoughts at all about this, I mean, any idea what could lie behind it?"

The Englishwoman was quick to respond.

"I haven't Mr Dolby, I haven't and this is the awful, the most galling thing. If we could have seen it coming, had some inkling, we might have been forewarned."

She stared intently ahead in a pose suggesting further information was lingering on her lips.

"Go on please Mrs MacManus."

"No, it's nothing. I just cannot believe anyone would have anything against Tim that's all. The boys loved him. He was always so kind and encouraging towards them all, irrespective of natural ability. He said there was something special to be captured and brought out in all children."

Mrs McManus seemed emotional and Zac wondered if he should withdraw and leave things for a day or two. "No. No we must be strong detective. Nothing was ever gained by giving up. One simply must come to terms with it for the sake of the school and the boys you understand?"

"Yes ma'am, of course."

Zac was quiet and respectful, which played well with the respectable Englishwoman suffering with dignity.

"Ah, tea and cake! Thank you Louisa."

Dealing adeptly with the paraphernalia of English tea she served the young foreigner as if he had been one of the boys from the school house. She had a motherly and practical manner, asking him quick unfussy questions about his preference for sugar and milk and such like.

Zac complied with the questions and instructions duly, as if indeed he had been an Eton Boy. He wasn't that much older than the boarders she kept a motherly eye on. She spoke again.

"She's Italian, this girl who came in with tea. Here on work experience and to improve her English. A very nice girl from a good family."

Zac straightened up from his plate.

"I guess it must be quite an opportunity for her working here, in this top-notch English school I mean?"

Silence for a second or two…

"You know there was something…"

Zac ignored being ignored. Mrs McManus was not a woman to be interrupted in her flow.

"Ma'am?"

"…something that happened about a week ago that I'd forgotten about until now."

"Is it to do with your husband?"

"Yes, it was to do with Tim now I come to think about it."

"Can you tell me what it was ma'am?"

Mrs MacManus leaned on the soft arm of her wing-chair, recalling events.

"It may be nothing, but the other day just after Chambers…"

His host detected a question in Zac's face.

"Yes, of course, how silly of me, you won't know what Chambers means.

It's a mid-morning break of twenty-five minutes when boys return to their houses for a snack, and masters have a chance to get together. Well, Tim had just finished up with his duties at Chambers, having an errand to run for me up at the top of Eton High Street. Nothing important, I wanted some fresh bread from the baker. They make their own bread and cakes freshly each day. That's one of theirs that you are eating at the moment Mr Dolby. Anyway, Tim was on his way back with the bread, and just before he turned off the High Street to come back into the house he bumped into a man."

"Someone he knew you mean?"

"No, not that kind of bumping into, Mr Dolby. I mean he actually collided with this man. It wasn't a huge thing. Tim was the soul of politeness, very old school, and he said (this is what he told me) *Oh, I do beg your pardon*. It sounds rather odd and stuffy these days I know, but you see that was how Tim was and everyone loved him for it."

"So was that all?"

"No actually detective, and this is why I mention it, and it's probably of no significance at all as I say. It turned out that this man was really quite aggressive towards him."

"Really? Did he threaten him?"

"No, Tim didn't say that, but apparently he said something strange for such an everyday occurrence."

"Go on."

"Sassenach!"

"Pardon me ma'am?"

"Sassenach. He called him a "Sassenach.""

"I… I'm sorry Mrs MacManus, but I…"

"You don't know what Sassenach means, you mean?"

Her voice sounded very faintly as though Zac had been caught not doing his homework."

"No ma'am, sorry I don't."

She looked at him kindly.

"It's a term used by the Scots for the English. It isn't especially polite. It actually goes back to the days of hostility between the Scots and the English. It means Saxon, or Lowlander."

"Oh OK, like Limey?"

"Yes, like Limey I suppose, or Yankee. That was used by the British to describe some of you Americans before the American Civil War."

Zac coloured and smiled all at once.

"I can see I don't know as much as I should about my own country's history Mrs MacManus."

The Englishwoman had moved on.

"Well the thing is, Tim is… or rather was, a history teacher and this word seemed to him like an attack against him. A direct hit he called it at the time. But he brushed it off of course."

"What did he mean a direct hit, ma'am?"

"Well, because this man was so nasty about it, because it was said here in Eton, because Tim was a history teacher and well yes, a Sassenach I suppose. But more particularly, because it sounded as though he was a Sassenach for someone for whom it meant something. It seemed so personal, the way he said it I mean. But as I said to Tim at the time, he couldn't have known him from Adam. We don't make a fuss over things Mr Dolby."

Zac thought for a second.

"This couldn't be some local guy?"

"Tim didn't think so. He said he'd never seen him before and he didn't see him again. After that he didn't mention the incident again and we forgot about it. As I say it's probably nothing. It just came to mind now because of what happened to Tim later on. The funny thing, the ironic thing, is that Tim wasn't as much of a Sassenach as all that."

"You mean he wasn't really English?"

"No not that exactly. He was English too, very English on the face of things. But he did have some long forgotten Scottish ancestry. I mean obviously the name MacManus for one thing. But there was more to it. If one goes back far enough, there are the trails of one's ancestry spreading like huge invisible tree roots back and back to who knows when or where? I mean do you know where your family are from originally Mr Dolby? Your name itself must come from somewhere."

Zac thought hard for a second.

"Well ma'am, my whole family are from Brooklyn. I guess I never really thought further back than that, tell you the truth. Oh, except for this one aunt from Michigan who's never mentioned."

Mrs MacManus smiled as though she hadn't noticed him speaking.

"Genealogy is fascinating and mysterious, Mr Dolby. You should look back into your own family's past- you may be surprised at what you find. Tim didn't know his own ancestry fully either and was, funnily enough, looking it up in the school library. The library is excellent here at Eton College. There are books on family histories going back centuries. I suppose he could have done it much quicker on the internet, but we feel more at ease with books at our age. Anyway, he said that he had some long overlooked Scottish roots but that he didn't know where they all went yet. He seemed very interested in it I must say."

Zac felt he should begin to wind things up.

"Thank you for so much helpful information ma'am. I really appreciate your time. It must be very difficult for you at this time and for the whole school. Can I ask that if you hear anything further or think of anything new regarding your husband's connection with this business, that you let me know?"

"Thank you Mr Dolby, yes naturally I shall, and thank you for this."

She held Zac's card up to the light to read his name and title. She looked as though she might be looking for a watermark. Her eye was sharp and discerning. She put it away in a pocket.

"I do hope we have been treating you kindly here detective. The British can be very stiff and starchy you know?"

"Oh I have been treated very kindly ma'am, I must say."

"Good and two pieces of cake suggest that you also enjoyed your English tea?"

Zac coloured again and nodded.

"Yes I did and thank you, very kind."

"So Mr Brydson, what happened next?"

The centre manager stared directly ahead.

"I just stood there looking at it… Like I say, I couldn't really take it in."

"Was anyone else around by now?"

"No sir, I was alone. I called my wife back pretty much straight away."

"What time?"

"It was recorded on my phone at 7.09am."

"Not the police first then? You called them at 7.10am."

Wylie's tone was insensitive.

"What my colleague means is did you not feel the police would've been the more obvious call to make first?"

Wylie turned a piercing eye on Abbi before moving on.

"Who was next on the scene Mr Brydson?"

"You know, I just don't remember. I'm sorry. I've been wracking my brain, but I just can't place who was there next after me."

Neither of the detectives liked this answer much. Abbi also felt it didn't add up.

"But surely you were aware of other people coming into the vicinity. After all you were in a heightened state of awareness Mr Brydson?"

"I would call it exactly a heightened state, miss. I'd say I was reeling from shock."

"Yes, but you said just now that you couldn't have missed the whole thing since it was so horrific?"

"Yes miss, but that was before I saw the amount of carnage there was. Everything was a mess… blood… gore… terrible. It sort of wiped my mind of other things if you know what I mean?"

Abbi nodded but without conviction. Something felt wrong. She just couldn't say what it was.

"OK, Mr Brydson, we know the police arrived at 7.20am. This was after a call made from your mobile. So d'you recall making the call and what was said?"

The centre manager sat upright in his chair appearing clearer on this point.

"Yes I do recall making the call. It's just the first five or ten minutes I'm struggling with. I'm sorry about that.

Wylie looked down at his notes nodding more to himself than anyone else. He wasn't happy though.

"Mr Brydson, what can you tell us about how the animal came to be there? You can't expect us to believe it appeared from nowhere. One moment there was nothing and then the next a scene of mayhem?"

"I'm not trying to tell you anything DI Wylie. I'm just saying what actually happened."

Again a vein of anger emerged towards the two detectives.

"Look I came here to try and help. I'm not under suspicion am I?"

Abbi looked over at him, searching his face and eyes for anything that may explain his reaction.

"No you're not here at this time, under caution or suspicion Mr Brydson. This is just to get to the facts. We may touch a nerve or two when we ask our questions, but this is to be expected in such a bizarre case. We hope that all members of the community will want to come forward to help in whatever ways they can. Do you not agree?"

This pacified the centre manager much less than previously.

"Yes I know, but please don't give me the bloody Queen's Speech about my duty as a loyal citizen. I've been through enough over the last few days."

Wylie's silence during this exchange was not passive. Abbi sensed he was angered but keeping his powder dry. He stood up and opened the door.

"We may need to see you again Mr Brydson. Thank you for coming in to see me."

Abbi noted the significance of the use of "to see me" but wasn't really surprised or bothered.

"Yes, goodbye for now Mr Brydson. We'll be getting expert analysis off the videotape from the mall soon, so we're quite likely to meet again."

The centre manager looked disgruntled as he left the interview room. Abbi concluded he wouldn't be saying anything more unless pushed.

Abbi arranged to meet Zac late that afternoon at the bar of The Two Brewers, an ancient traditional pub situated by the gates to the Long Walk. She didn't like the landlord but it was a nice pub. She waved at him through the low-slung pub windows, breezing in and up close.

"So what happened in Eton?"

Zac felt her closeness with pleasure.

"Oh I met the widow. She's cool. She gave me cake."

Zac was pleased to see Abbi. They were now completely relaxed together. He hadn't forgotten her strange departure from the curry-house of course, but thought he would wait for her to come back to it when or if she felt like it.

"Giving young foreign men cake is high up on MI5's list of dangerous behaviour I hear."

"It's handy I work for the FBI then, Miss Matilda."

They grinned at each other, easy with the banter.

"But seriously what did she tell you, the widow?"

"Well her husband had a peculiar meeting with some guy a few days prior to his death."

Zac traded the Eton encounter for Abbi's tetchy Wylie and Brydson encounter.

"So really as far as the swan incident is concerned, we're no further on?"

Abbi looked thoughtful.

"We really need that videotape analysis. The whole thing has the look of a conjuring trick about it at the moment. Does Pawley know anything more about the tapes?"

Abbi checked her mobile.

"I had a call from Reading a few hours ago and I need to call them back. I guess it's about time for a major recap and debriefing. Pawley will be on the war-path unless things start to come together soon. We had better get Wylie to put together what he knows before we go over to Reading."

Zac smirked.

"Sure won't take long for Wylie to do that."

Abbi pushed him playfully.

"You shouldn't underestimate Wylie. He can be pretty tricky if you get on the wrong side of him."

"Sounds like you know that from personal experience."

Abbi stayed quiet.

"Do you know anything?"

She deflected him.

"The Eton thing. The Sassenach comment, what do you reckon?"

Zac considered.

"I don't know. I mean to you guys I'm a Yank I guess, but I don't hear that used in a bad way. It sounds kinda friendly to me."

"Yank *is* friendly. We like you. As I recall you've helped us out of some tricky situations."

She smiled impishly...

"...Albeit a little unpunctually. Then during the war you Yanks were our saviours: rich and powerful and most of all... on *our* side. I mean you *are* us in many ways, our descendants I mean."

Abbi's mobile interrupted her.

"It's about the Reading meet, tomorrow, exact time to follow."

"Who?"

"You, me, Wylie, Pawley and the video tech guy. It's a feedback session first and then we'll go through the tape fully."

"Does Wylie have the forensics?"

"Don't know. If he remembers his own name he's usually having a good day."

Zac listened more seriously as she continued.

"The thing is, up to now we've had nothing in the way of forensic evidence whatsoever. Whoever's doing this barbaric stuff is very careful and very clever."

"So it can't be Wylie then!"

Zac liked his own wisecrack but was immediately silenced by the look on his English partner's face. Abbi looked away.

"Listen, I'm sorry Abbi. Clearly I've said something wrong here. Do you want to talk about it?"

Abbi looked him straight in the eyes.

"Not yet Zac, maybe never, but certainly not yet."

"Is this why you left the curry-house the other day?"

Zac could see that for now the subject was closed. Abbi was looking down at her phone in place of replying.

"Look, the text-god is confirming the time of the Reading meeting tomorrow. 10am on the dot."

Zac dropped the subject of Wylie for now.

Chapter Nine

Reading Police HQ was particularly grim-looking. The summer had been a washout anyway, but this late August day was especially cold and it had been drizzling since dawn. Abbi and Zac made their way to the large incident room towards the car-park end of the faceless grey police building. George Pawley looked grey too, sitting upright and grave at the front of the room, waving people to sit down until all the numbers were complete. He then stood up.

"OK this is the plan."

Everyone was instantly hushed. George Pawley had a powerful presence and a voice of deep gravity. It made him magnetic to watch and listen to.

"We will hear from Detectives Matilda and Dolby about main areas of progress in the case, followed by DI Wylie regarding forensics from both crime scenes of Slough and Eton. Then we will hear about the all-important technical analysis of the tape from Queensmere Shopping Centre. That will be covered by John Bream. First let me set the scene."

His voice already grave, took on a yet more sombre tone.

"Some days ago at the Queensmere Shopping Centre in Slough, a Mute Swan was butchered in a particularly disturbing and sadistic manner. It was and is I believe the work of a deviant mind. We now know that the swan was from her Majesty The Queen's own flock that live on the Thames in Windsor. The questions I pose now are for further investigation please. How was this animal taken? How did it get from Windsor to Slough? How did it get in to the shopping arcade? How did it appear, apparently from nowhere, in the state in which it was found? I hope that the analysis of the videotape will help with this last question, but the whole movement and killing of the animal is of a piece, and I want to know the whole story, clear?"

Nobody answered since it was a largely rhetorical question. George Pawley wanted to know; ergo it was their job to find out. Pawley drove on with his delivery.

"Right, turning to the matter of Timothy MacManus, a housemaster from Eton College – a seemingly more significant matter."

Pawley stopped momentarily to look over the small audience in front of him. Satisfied that to the last man and woman they were paying rapt attention, he went on.

"I say a seemingly more significant matter ... because this was a human being after all, not an animal. But I urge you not to consider these two events in isolation. As I said just now we're looking at the work of a very sick mind. This investigation is deadly serious and nobody should forget it. The swan was and is, for the purposes of the investigation, equal in significance to the death of the man, even though naturally, the man's murder is more serious per se. What we are seeking to understand here is the self-evidently cruel and sinister intention behind both events."

He gestured to Abbi and Zac to stand up and walk to the front.

"Now we'll hear from DI Matilda and Lieutenant Zachery Dolby, who is on secondment from New York's Police Department in the US. Please pay close attention to what they have to say, thank you."

Abbi was nervous but collected herself quickly.

"Hi. Greetings to all our colleagues. We want to bring you up to speed on events starting from the discovery of the unfortunate swan in Slough, and take you through the investigation up to the present. Lieutenant Dolby and I will each speak regarding that part we have each covered, either together or separately, in this case so far."

Zac shifted very slightly in his chair at the mention of his name. He was really quite nervous at the idea of addressing an all British police team, but inwardly reassured by Abbi's presence. Abbi was still speaking.

"On Tuesday August 26th I was called by Chief Superintendent Pawley to attend an incident in Slough. I had no idea what was fully involved until I was at the scene. Lieutenant Dolby and I made initial contact with DI Wylie who was already at the scene of crime. A number of uniformed officers and SOCO's were already in attendance. The first impression of the scene was that of butchery, there's no other way to describe it. The bird, a Mute Swan, technically the property of the Crown, had been bled to death by the slitting of its throat. But there the gory part ends. The body had been arranged with its wings aloft in the form of an arc with the tips of the wings meeting at the apex. The image it created was of a fallen angel.

The audience had been very still and quiet. Now a single hand went up.

"How were the wings kept "aloft" as you put it?"

"They were tied with a plastic tie and a short thick wooden stake jammed underneath."

Another hand, another question.

"Where was this torture instrument you mentioned, and what was it again?"

"The medieval instrument of torture used was one designed to tear the flesh of females considered to have committed adultery. They are a pair of sharp tongues. The name of the device is a Breast-Ripper. It was about four feet from the dead bird."

"So this instrument was used to kill the bird?"

Abbi responded.

"We assume so, although there was no useful outside forensic evidence I know of. Maybe we'll hear more now from one of my colleagues.

"Was there anything else DI Matilda?"

87

"Yes, there was we understand, a postcard-sized picture of a mother swan with two young. DI Wylie has been in charge of this aspect of the case. He'll tell us more on this subject shortly I expect."

Zac shifted in his chair sensing that it was now his turn.

"Lieutenant Zac Dolby will now tell us more about the Timothy MacManus killing and his meeting with his widow in Eton."

Zac rose.

"Dear respected colleagues and new friends. My name is Lieutenant Zachery Dolby. I normally work out of Brooklyn in the New York Police Department, NYPD for short. I have to thank you for your warm welcome here in England for an upstart Yank."

The small audience seemed to like this friendly opening.

"The truth is that this has come as a shock to me in more ways than one. This whole business is bizarre and mysterious. But more than this I figure it presents us with a number of elements and oppositions: the modern versus the ancient, the Crown versus the Commoner, tradition versus the upstart."

It seemed to the room that Zac, self-proclaimed upstart Yank, had a way with words. He developed his theme.

"The elements and oppositions I speak of in these ominous events are apparent to me not in spite of my being an outsider here, but *because* I'm an outsider. This is the entire point of departure for me in this case. I was shipped out here just over a week ago from a city only numbering a few decades of modern existence into a world going back for centuries. You Brits may not see the relevance of this, but I can tell you there is relevance. What I mean basically is that I notice things that you may take for granted."

One of the audience wanted to know what this may be.

"Such as, Mr Dolby?"

"Such as your complete acceptance of history and tradition and how they figure in your lives. Also, I guess your acceptance of the social status quo. You're immersed in your own past and wedded to tradition. Because you *belong* so totally, I figure you just may have become blind towards what's in front of you."

Some of the audience looked sceptical, perhaps irked at this Zac noticed.

"OK, let me ask you something. How many of you last really noticed the town that you work in?"

"Where exactly do you mean lieutenant?"

"Windsor, or Slough or Reading come to that?"

Those who worked Windsor seemed ready to meet this challenge.

"What have you noticed that I haven't?"

"Thank you er..."

"DI Penry."

"Thank you DI Penry. To answer your question, let me first ask you a couple. What is currently the highest point of Windsor Castle?"

"The flag pole."

Some laughter.

"No, currently there's work being carried out on the Round Tower of the castle and the boom of a crane is currently the highest point."

George Pawley looked impressed.

"OK so where does the band march from and to?"

"The Barracks to the castle, and back again".

"Sure, usually you'd be correct. Only currently the band cannot march that route because of gas mains work cutting off Windsor High Street for two weeks."

Pawley stood up.

"OK Lieutenant, quite impressive, but what's the net product of your insights?"

"Well sir, at present there is nothing concrete to show for it, but I hope to use fresh eyes to help take this case forward. This is my central contribution sir, new eyes."

Pawley countered.

"Ok, that's all very well and good, but tell us what you've come up with through actual as opposed to hopeful detective work."

Zac wasn't going to talk back to George Pawley, and saw that it was time to say what he'd done up to now.

"Yes of course sir. Well I accompanied DI Matilda to Eton to view the scene of the murder of Mr Timothy MacManus. There are a number of areas for further investigation there. The body of the ill-fated Eton House-Master was found in the old stocks, located in front of the Cockpit Italian Restaurant. Stocks are an ancient contraption where the victim is clamped hands and feet into wooden restraints, kind of like being cuffed. It's more a medieval punishment than a torture thing. But in this case this guy MacManus was also suffocated with a plastic bag. The bag was placed over his head, tightened, and held there until he asphyxiated. But the most powerful aspect to the whole thing was that he'd had a turnip forced into his mouth. From where I'm standing this was done to mock the guy. It was real personal. What's more, on the body we found another of those white cards like the one picked up in Slough on the dead bird. It had some Latin writing on it which DI Amy Joss has kindly translated for us. The meaning goes something like: *courage is greater through adversity.* We're also hoping some forensics will show up to help us out."

Zac cast a glance over at Wylie who didn't look his way, or indeed any way, but sat very stonily at the back of the room.

Zac finished off.

"DI Matilda and I hooked up at the scene with the police pathologist, Mr John Courtenay. The body of Mr MacManus was still being processed. Like I say we await further news."

"Any others areas either of you two want to tell us about?"

George Pawley searched the two young DI's with his probing dark eyes.

Abbi stood back up.

"Yes sir. Lieutenant Dolby and I visited Windsor Guildhall Museum as part of our research in to the kind of torture instruments involved in this case. We understand from the museum curator that a packing case was due to be opened that may have contained some other examples of these vicious antique devices. However just now I received a phone call from him saying that there was, in the end, nothing of interest in the packing case."

Pawley looked over sharply.

"And you accepted that at face value did you?"

His tone for once betrayed a touch of anger.

"Well yes sir."

"Well, Miss Matilda, and Mister Dolby, I suggest you do not take it as such. Go back and ask more questions. I'm most diverted by the notion of your new eyes Lieutenant Dolby, but we still await the product of them. The only way to see anything with new eyes or any eyes come to that, is to go and look!"

Zac and Abbi marked his words in respectful silence.

"Now, DI Wylie, your turn to speak."

"Yes sir."

Wylie looked nervously at Pawley's summons, edging his way to the front of the room.

"So hello and welcome to everyone, DI Wylie, Thames Valley. I also attended the crime scene involving the er… bird in Queensmere, and also attended the scene of the murdered History Master in Eton, prior to the other two detectives. I have been looking in to the forensics at both scenes and also interviewed the Queensmere centre manager, Mr James Brydson. I'm afraid to report that there's literally no forensics at either crime scene. I've been in close contact with the police pathologist, Mr John Courtenay, and the forensics team who covered both scenes of crime. They confirm no suspect forensic material has yet been discovered."

George Pawley looked philosophical.

"Is there anything you have been able to detect, detective?"

Wylie didn't miss the ironic phraseology of the question, but ploughed on.

"The centre manager says that he saw nothing of any significance except the crime scene itself. I feel though that he still has more to give. We really need to see him again."

"Anything else DI Wylie?"

"Yes sir. I have this. I think DI Matilda mentioned it already.

Wylie held up the postcard-sized illustration of the swan with her young, found under the dead animal's wing. He held it tentatively up for those at the front to see. In his movements he gave a sense that it was a kind of consolation for not having anything else of any use to report.

"Can everyone see it?"

George Pawley's strong, compelling voice provoked a few people to go forward to take a closer look. Abbi was amongst them. She spoke out softly, almost to herself.

"Those are *not* swans."

Pawley looked over at her, soldering his gaze together with hers.

"Oh? What are they DI Matilda?"

"I am a history major sir. Those birds on the card are actually called Pelican Argents. They represent a heraldic symbol. I forget exactly which one, but they're definitely not swans."

George Pawley looked over at Wylie who had sat back down seeking obscurity.

"OK another matter for speedy investigation DI Matilda, since you're the history major."

Pawley made this a cut-off comment, clearly keen to move on to the video analysis.

"Can we hear from the videotape expert?"

A voice:

"Yes sir."

A young thin man made his way rapidly to the front at Pawley's gruff instruction.

"Hi everyone. John Bream. I'm an independent video technician specialising in deconstructing and analysing videotapes and their contents for the police. My aim in this case was to prove, if possible, the integrity of the tape in question, the machine used to record it, and most importantly, the authenticity of the footage. By that I mean that the tape viewed is indeed the actual one from the machine used at that time and that location. Also that the footage is an accurate and true reflection of what transpired."

Again Pawley pushed the process doggedly forward.

"Go ahead Mr Bream."

"Yes sir. OK all the processes I went through, and without getting too technical, show that the tape I analysed is in fact the authentic tape taken from the camera at Queensmere Shopping Centre on the day and time in question. It is a so-called continuous-loop tape. This particular one runs for exactly two and a half hours, then rewinds and tapes over the previous time period."

The audience again were inquisitive.

"So what'll it show?"

"It'll show, unless anyone paused or stopped the machine, the last period of up to two and a half hours to the point that it was stopped for analysis. This time was 10am."

"So it may only show some of the period under investigation in this case?"

"True."

Another question:

"Does it show if it was stopped or paused?"

"That is something I cannot answer conclusively. This machine just doesn't have the sophistication."

"So if it was stopped or paused, the tape may show footage that is out of time sequence?"

"Yes it's possible. But there's nothing on the tape showing disjointed parts or actions. My guess is that it wasn't stopped during its normal recording process."

"Does the tape record the whole mall?"

"No, it is positioned to view whatever lies in a straight line from one end of the mall to the other and only in one direction. The camera will show everything oncoming from the south end of the centre to the north end. But anyone walking south to north away from the camera will be seen from behind only. Also it cannot see round corners, if I can put it this way."

Another hand went up.

"What about the crucial moment? The exact moment when the swan wasn't there and then it was?"

All ears and eyes were on the tech guy.

"Right this is where we have more of a problem." Pawley also looked at him intently. It was enough to rouse John Bream to continue quickly.

"The swan is not in evidence at 7.02am but is there in full gory detail at 7.08am."

"And?"

"And… well I can't actually explain it."

The audience started to get restless.

"Right so we get you here to give us nothing concrete?"

"Well I'm sorry, but there really is nothing to see. You can look for yourself."

Pawley intervened.

"OK in that case, can you please show us the tape Mr Bream?"

The technician turned to the screen in front of him and clicked. The scene unfolded very much as the centre manager had reported. The tape's quality was pretty poor and in black and white. Black and white somewhat grainy tapes made everybody involved in the footage look like criminals by definition, but the sequence of the centre manager's routine movements from the north to the south of the shopping mall, made for uneventful viewing. The postman is seen greeting the centre manager just after 7am. The tape wound on and Mr Bream looked at the video counter to see that as he approached the key moment, he could talk everyone through it.

"Here's the centre manager speaking on his mobile. A call came in from his wife I understand. We can see at first he has his back to the critical area where the animal's yet to appear, he's facing north, being filmed by the camera at the southern end of the shopping centre."

The tape moved frame by frame as the video expert sought to demonstrate to his audience that he had done his job fully and properly.

"Ok so here're the frames immediately prior to the animal's appearance."

The mall looked empty, and the centre manager was just closing his conversation with his wife and beginning to turn round to face the onlooking video camera.

"Now, in this frame we see nothing, but in the following one the scene's utterly different."

Some in the audience gasped as the full bloody facts of the scene simply appeared before them. The swan was in the exact positon in which it had been discovered by the stunned Mr Brydson. To be fair to the centre manager, as you viewed him in the footage, did look pale and transfixed. The tape continued running, showing the first police arriving on the scene.

Pawley's voice:

"I notice that Mr Brydson is out of shot some of the time after first discovering the scene until the police arrive. His explanation apparently is that he needed to sit down because of the shock before getting on the phone to his wife again and then onto the police?"

John Bream:

"Yes that's correct sir."

George Pawley stood up and paced about.

"So Mr Bream, you say you find the tape to be authentic and completely free from tampering?"

"Yes sir."

"Can you break down the frames any further to see how this apparition gets there?"

"No sir, there simply is no obvious moment of appearance."

"Damned illogical. It looks like a conjuring trick to me!"

George Pawley sounded irritable. His long career in policing had not made him keen on the unexplainable.

"Ok Mr Bream, let's look at the footage again. Please can everyone pay close attention in case we're missing something here?"

Pawley reigned over a room of loyal police subjects. They all fell silent and focused intently on the tape. Mr Bream as before, ran very slowly frame by frame through the critical moments up to the moment of the swan's ghostly appearance. A hush hung on after the viewing as people digested the scene again.

"There is a kind of wobble there."

Zac's words aroused no immediate comment, but a few heads turned to look at him. He wasn't sure if the looks he received were just blank or possibly faintly negative. Nobody else seemed to think anything worthy of comment. The room fell silent again pending the judgement of the sage, grey-haired George Pawley.

Abbi looked over at Zac questioningly, whispering.

"How do you mean, *a wobble*?"

"The last frame before the bird appears has a kind of wobble to it. It's a bit like when you throw a rock into water. If you wait a few seconds the ripples nearly fade out, but in the final few seconds, milliseconds, there's a tiny distortion on the surface – a kind of wannabe ripple. That's what it reminds me of on the tape in the frame before the bird's appearance. Nobody else saw it though, so maybe I'm just seeing things"

Abbi looked at him without judgement. She didn't know if there was anything in what he was saying, but thought she'd accept it for the time being. She wanted him to feel she took his opinion seriously.

"Seeing things is our job Zac. Let's try and look over the tape on our own after this winds up."

Zac appreciated her faith in him.

"OK sure. We can go up and see the Bream guy when the ugly mob has dispersed."

There was a bond of friendship between them.

Abbi touched his arm softly.

"Look, I want to talk to you about another couple of things that have been bugging me, especially after Pawley's beef about the museum. Let's go over to Windsor Guildhall first thing tomorrow and ask more questions."

"Right. I don't want any grief with Pawley that's for sure. D'you reckon he's pinning it on us for not chasing up the museum guy?"

"He probably blames you lieutenant. How could anyone blame me?"

Abbi smiled innocently and stuck out a pretty pink tongue.

"Yes ma'am. Who indeed?!"

Pawley was finishing off with words of stern encouragement.

"Get stuck in please ladies and gents. I don't want any more deaths on my watch!"

The meeting began to break up. They were to be disappointed however in their hopes of viewing the videotape in private. Mr Bream had departed rapidly after the meeting broke up, as had Wylie. Both seemed keen to avoid any further grilling from George Pawley.

Chapter Ten

"Hello again detectives!"

The museum curator was chirpy.

"Hello sir. We thought we'd drop in just to talk over the matter of what was in that packing case."

Again the man was loud and jolly.

"Or *not* in it, DI Matilda!"

"Well yes, Detective Dolby and I were intrigued. First you were certain that there were more artefacts from medieval times, maybe even torture instruments and then, nothing at all?"

The curator smiled.

"Oh no, not nothing, just not what we were hoping for!"

"Sir?"

"Yes lieutenant?"

"What we need to understand is why you thought the goods in that trunk were medieval sir, only to smoke it out as a bunch of other stuff entirely? Please tell us what the deal was with the trunk in the end."

The curator was very pleased to be asked questions. He motioned them to a long polished, hard wooden bench so he could cover the matter thoroughly.

"Please detectives, come and sit down on my long throne."

He chuckled.

"It would make a good place for a coronation, this grand room, don't you think?"

Abbi and Zac sat down and waited for more sensible conversation to break out.

"I'm pretty sure it said medieval devices on the docket, but I'll have to double-check. I suppose I must have wondered what else it could be except a box full of wonderfully nasty things, that's all. In the end it was a big disappointment."

The curator wore a look of ghoulish enthusiasm. Zac continued.

"Sir can you just run through things really carefully and slowly since we last met?"

"Yes of course lieutenant. When you were last here I think I mentioned to you both that I was waiting for a colleague to help me open a newly delivered packing case, and that we undertake this with a minimum of two staff, for both security and museum protocol. We have to make sure that all items are double-checked, verified as authentic, and itemised in the official museum catalogue."

Abbi encouraged more information.

"So you were surprised by the contents of the case?"

"As I said…"

The curator seemed very slightly irked by the repeated question. Something in his manner implied that he was the expert, and not in need of leading in the right direction.

"…As I said at the time the paperwork indicated there were various medieval items, some of which I imagined to be torture instruments. You can understand how disappointing it was when we only found some Edwardian tat!"

"What exactly was it sir?"

The curator leered over at Zac with luridly blue zealous eyes.

"Well you Americans might have been excited by it!"

Zac didn't react to this.

"It was just tat."

"Yes, but what exactly sir?"

"I've a list here Miss Matilda."

He passed Abbi a long perforated piece of A4 paper.

She shared it with Zac. Silence for approximately forty seconds.

"Is this everything?"

"Yes miss."

Zac was still looking though the list.

"May we see these items sir?"

The curator was excited.

"Yes, of course you may! So long as you're both OK to get rather dusty?"

Turning on his heel he beckoned them on skittishly, leading the way down to the museum's storage area in the large cellar. The atmosphere was damp and smelled of camphor.

"Mothballs," the curator shouted back at them.

"There's quite a quantity of garments and fabrics down here that we need to protect."

Zac picked his way past items that went back centuries, way before the modern era of North America that he hailed from.

"Where do these packing trunks come from sir?"

"They come from various places lieutenant."

"This one we'll be viewing here though, who sent it?"

"I'll check for you. I think it came direct from the castle itself. When we get back to civilisation I'll look at the docket."

"I'm obliged sir."

"Oh, no problem lieutenant, anything for the NYPD!"

Again the curator chuckled as if at a private joke.

They arrived at a packing case very much like tens of others in the dusty storage facility. The curator stopped comically sharp and stood up very straight, like a child pretending to be a soldier.

"Aha! Now then number sixty-two let's be 'aving you!"

They waited for him to cut the official museum tags, going through a careful process to show the case had been opened correctly, and not tampered with.

"We will have to put new seals on these when we finish and do the entries. The procedure is very strict."

Abbi supplied recognition of his efforts.

"Yes of course. Thank you for taking all this trouble."

"No trouble, no trouble!"

His loud zealous voice echoed around the dusty store rooms.

"I enjoy all of this you know!"

The contents of the packing case were disappointing, and reflected what the museum curator had said they were. Abbi noted the collection of Edwardian artefacts as they were brought out: letters from a duchess to a duke, some ivory fans from India, a couple of large floral ladies' hats, (taking up most of the box) and a few silver coins of Persian origin. The three people looked at each other blankly for a few seconds until Abbi straightened up and looked at her watch.

"Can you let us see the docket please sir?"

"Yes of course Detective Matilda. Shall we go back up for air?"

He seemed to have enjoyed the wild goose chase quite well as they opened the door back into the Guildhall Museum itself.

"The paperwork sir, did it come together with the trunk, or under a separate cover?"

The curator tutted to himself as if Zac should have known better than to ask such a question.

"The paperwork always comes together with the packing cases lieutenant; it means that the paper-trail is complete. Disjointed paperwork makes things messy! Right, now for that docket."

Having emerged, only slightly dusty, from the museum's innards, the curator went to a drawer in his small office which formed a mere bite of space out of the resplendent Guildhall Museum, and opened a filing cabinet. He rummaged for a full minute. When he came back he looked quite different to the preceding twenty minutes they had shared with him. He'd lost his bright manner.

"This is really quite awful!"

"Sir?"

"Well Miss Matilda, sorry DI Matilda I should say. The docket for that packing case has disappeared, literally disappeared!"

"Sir we need to verify the facts. This could put the brakes on our investigation. Can you get hold of a copy?"

"Yes lieutenant, I'll get onto it straight away, straight away! I really am sorry about this. I just don't know what could've happened."

The museum curator seemed genuine in his distress. There was real panic behind eyes betraying how perturbing he found this blip in his perfectly organised world. This man was an oddity certainly, but he gave off the sense of being exactly what he was, odd but genuine. This was their current assessment anyway.

"OK sir, please let us know the instant you have the copy docket."

"Yes miss I will."

Some few minutes later in the foyer of Windsor Police Station, Abbi and Zac parted company to get online.

"Research beckons, lieutenant."

"Too right, see you later Miss Matilda."

Chapter Eleven

DI Wylie arrived at the office of the Swan Protection Society located just by the River Thames. His target for questioning shook his hand firmly. Wylie liked this. A man with a firm handshake could be trusted in his book.

"Mr Trite?"

"Yes. DI Wylie?"

"Yes sir, I need to ask you a few questions about the birds er... the swans in particular, on the Thames, here in Windsor."

"Very happy to help detective, what d'you want to know?"

"You've heard about the incident in Slough I suppose Mr Trite?"

"Yes terrible, that was George."

Wylie looked baffled.

"The swan in question was called George. He's about the fourth or fifth George we've had over the years. Yes, it was definitely George."

"Oh, I see. How d'you know it was that bird in particular Mr Trite?"

Mr Trite looked out over the River Thames thoughtfully.

"The thing is all the Mute Swans in open water on the Thames are the property of Her Majesty the Queen. She can claim any birds she wishes. Long ago swans were eaten as a great delicacy. She doesn't really exercise her rights over them much these days of course."

"But how d' you know the swan in question was one called George sir?"

Still unfocused Mr Trite rattled on.

"Oh yes sorry, I get a bit carried away on the subject of swans when I get started. Have you heard of swan-upping Detective?"

He didn't wait for any confirmation before going on again. Swan-upping is the annual census of the swan population on stretches of the Thames in a number of the Home Counties including Berkshire. It's a ceremony dating from the 12th century when, as I said, the Crown could claim ownership of all Mute Swans. As you can imagine we have close ties with the swan-upping ceremony and we name the swans that we recognise. So we know this was George."

Wylie was anxious to home in on the facts before the man got carried away again.

"So how could the animal have found its way to Slough? Could it have flown there?"

Mr Trite looked back at him blankly.

"Why would George go to Slough?"

Wylie had a sense that the conversation was becoming a touch surreal.

He resisted the temptation in his growing irritation to say something like *for a wider range of shops*.

"I was hoping you could help me out on that sir."

Mr Trite looked at the policeman as if he may've been cornered by a dangerous imbecile.

"No I don't think there's anything in Slough for a swan. They need water and the sanctuary of the river, and they like to stick to their own. Now I suppose if the ducks started going over there…"

Wylie stopped him.

"Sir a crime has been committed and a nasty one at that. We want to get to the bottom of what could've happened to the bird in question from the time it was last seen here on the river, to when it came to grief in Queensmere."

Mr Trite nodded gravely.

"You do know it's considered an offence to kill a wild Mute Swan since – as I was just saying - they're considered to be property of the Crown? Also they're protected under the Wildlife and Countryside Act of 1981. Killing or injuring a swan used to be classed as treason under a law dating back to the 12th century."

Wylie was faintly impressed by this account. He liked the law and facts relating to it, and the notion of treason against the Crown made him both cross and also excited.

"Ok then sir, let's look at this differently. Can you tell me when you last saw... er, George?"

"Yes I certainly can tell you that."

A moment or so passed. Wylie with some effort of will remained calm.

"Yes sir?"

"Oh, yes of course."

Mr Trite juddered in to life.

"I would have seen him the night before he died."

"How can you be sure of that sir?"

"Because I always come down here to the river of an evening to check on them. I'm here all weathers and every day of the year. I see it as a kind of duty to Her Majesty herself if you know what I mean?"

"There must be huge numbers of swans on the river though sir. How d'you know it was this particular one? They're all tagged with serial numbers I believe?

Trite nodded.

"Yes, they're all tagged. But the thing is George also has, I mean had, a slight kink in his neck. You couldn't miss him. It was the result of an operation to remove a fish-hook from his throat about two years ago. It was one of these damned rogue anglers of course, just discarding their lines any bloody where they feel like it. If I could've caught the little swine!"

The man's face went red with anger and quite contorted almost out of recognition for a few moments. The veins in his neck stood out like green wire.

Wylie asserted himself.

"Can we just stick to the facts please sir?"

"Yes of course, sorry."

"What I need to know is if anyone could've taken the bird, and if they did, when it could have happened?"

Mr Trite seemed clear of his facts on this.

"I left at 9ish on that evening so I suppose any time between 9pm approximately and the next day before he was found in that... well... that state."

Mt Trite was clearly upset at revisiting the thought of the swan's cruel exit from the world.

"Can I ask if anyone else takes such a great interest as you do in the flock here?"

"No detective, nobody's as close as I am to the birds."

"Anyone you can think of that may have harboured a grudge against the swans or their royal connection?"

Again the swan-lover looked at the policeman as if he may be in need of psychiatric help.

"Who'd 'ave it in for my swans?"

Wylie looked a little trapped, and couldn't think of a plausible answer to this question.

Trite continued with some passion.

"Especially George, he'd had a terrible time of it. I mean you just had to look at the expression in his eyes to see how much he'd been through. My poor George."

"They are Her Majesty's swans sir."

"Yes sorry, The Queen's swans, though she can't possibly know them or love them as I do!"

His tone was resentful of any suggestion that someone might be more loyal to the Mute Swans than he. Wylie noted the bird enthusiast's manner carefully and made a mental note of his strange behaviour.

"I may need to come back at some point Mr Trite. Thank you for your time. Oh one more thing before I go. Does the Swan Protection Society produce postcards with pictures of swans or other birds on, for sale or distribution?"

Mr Trite was clear on this.

"No, not at all. The only postcards are sold by the Tourist Board. They don't have any bird ones though or I'd know about it."

"OK, thanks again Mr Trite. I'll be in touch."

"What the..."

Zac felt almost faint at the news. This fairy-tale castle-town was fast becoming a surreal kingdom of wicked witches and evil goblins.

Abbi's voice on his cell was speaking to thin air while Zac was reeling from the news.

"Jeez, when did this happen?"

Abbi for her part sounded clear-headed and solemn.

"Meet me at the gates to the Long Walk in half an hour."

"Sure. OK."

Zac arrived at the ornate gates to the Long Walk just under half an hour later to find Abbi in conversation with Wylie. Wylie viewed him sourly.

"You turned up eventually then?"

"Yes I was researching mirrors."

"You what?"

Wylie looked at the American as if he had lost his mind.

"This case must've gone to your head. I've been doing some real police work over on the Thames, and DI Matilda here's at the sharp end with another gruesome topping."

Zac didn't feel it was necessary to explain himself to Wylie and instead moved over to Abbi to get more details.

"What gives?"

"Well DI Wylie's correct about another gruesome murder I'm afraid. The Pub Landlord this time, Archie McCredie. An unlikable character by all accounts, but still a nasty end for anyone."

Zac's voice was low and serious.

"What's the story?"

Wylie was keen to display his knowledge.

"The Landlord was found this afternoon at 3pm. He was behind the bar next to a cask of sherry. His head was flat as a pancake. Another of those old torture devices was used."

"Thanks Wylie, I can probably give a more technical account myself."

"Yes DI Matilda I expect you can sex it up for us."

"I suppose I might not confuse the instrument used with a tennis racquet, or a Pelican Argent, Wylie but then maybe I'm better informed than that."

Wylie shut up suddenly sensing he was on his way to a hiding if he pushed it.

Abbi resumed.

"The device used this time's called a Head Crusher. The head's placed under an upper metal cap and the chin placed above the bottom bar. A screw mechanism on the top's slowly turned, compressing the skull tightly. First the teeth go, and then the jaw's shattered and splintered. After that the eyes are squeezed from the sockets. In the end, the skull fractures and the contents of the head are forced out. It's the most horrible thing."

Zac stood motionless, clearly rattled by the news.

"Shall we take a look?"

Abbi put a restraining hand on the eager American detective.

"I've already seen him, and I don't recommend a viewing if you can avoid it."

Zac took her at her word. His sleep had been erratic recently and he was feeling delicate. Wylie interrupted again, keen to update them about background he had found out on the swan. Zac paid attention. He didn't like Wylie but he was a professional and a colleague.

"So in the end we still don't know how the swan got to Slough?"

"No but this guy is one major weirdo I can tell you. If anyone had anything against his swans, this guy could be dangerous."

"Do you think he could have something to do with it himself?"

"No. Not necessarily Lieutenant Dolby, not yet anyway. Over here we don't just charge in like cops off the telly. We do the groundwork first."

Abbi looked over at Zac with a don't-even-bother-he's-just-an-idiot look. Again it was good enough for Zac.

They went up by train early the next day to Reading to see George Pawley.

"Still no forensics!?" Pawley was pretty worked up this time.

"How can we get anywhere when we've nothing to go on? Anyway who was this last guy? What's his name?"

Abbi looked at her notes. "Archie McCredie. He was Landlord of the Two Brewers. It's an ancient pub that stands right up next to the Long Walk sir."

"A Scot?"

Abbi nodded.

"It would appear so sir."

"Detective Dolby, what do you make of all this?"

Zac straightened his back visibly as George Pawley glared at him.

"I see the hand of history in it sir."

George Pawley simply amplified his glare.

"What I mean sir is that… well..."

"More of your elements and oppositions, detective?"

"Actually yes sir. There seem to be some really clear if mysterious themes in this case."

Pawley looked plainly irritated.

"Is that not a contradiction Mr Dolby, clear *and* mysterious?"

"No not really. What I'm saying is that the manner of killing is gruesome and also cryptic, but it's still consistent. The instruments used are from the medieval era, and the people involved are all what I would term indigenous."

Zac could see that he'd have to be more convincing to win over the gruff and seasoned policeman.

"Ok, take the swan sir. The bird was the victim of a killing with a message. We need to find out what the message was. I figure it's something to do with the background to the bird itself. What it stands for. We know that swans have a royal connection. But then we've got the mixed message of the other bird sketch found under the wing of the dead bird. It is a large white bird, but not a swan. I don't think that the killer was confused like Wylie was. I feel sure this guy knows the difference between the two types of bird. What's more, with MacManus the card with the Latin on it must have an obvious message to it. We just gotta join up the dots somehow."

Pawley listened more closely.

"Proceed Mr Dolby."

Pawley was beginning to soften slightly, feeling that just possibly this Yank could get somewhere with his off-beam thinking.

"So Mr MacManus, the Eton housemaster - he's another indigenous kind of guy. He's right in the blood vessels of this joint. He's also working in the place that's buried in the past of the area, this famous public school Eton. Now we know he's in some kind of hassle with this one guy; a guy who's already mad at him. The only problem is we don't know why the guy's mad at him. All we know is there's something coded in the name he calls him. Right, so then we have the slaying of the pub landlord, Mr Archie McCredie, another guy who's in like the fabric of the town. He knows everyone and plenty of people thought he was a schmuck. But, again there's a link in the method of his killing. Pawley looked irritated again.

"But even an eleven-year-old child could see that, Mr Dolby. The medieval instrument theme is staring us in the face. In fact I thought you were interviewing this museum curator again?"

Abbi moved an arm nervously.

"We have sir, I'll tell you about it."

Zac was still eager to complete his circle of logic.

"What I guess I mean sir is that there's more to this than just the wacko gadgets used in the killings, more than just oddball messages- the sketch of the Pelican Argent, the card with the Latin, – there's something from the past trying to connect with us here."

Pawley sighed a long tired sigh.

"OK, you two need to track down this element or ghost or whatever it is. We don't need any further deaths in such a small, and may I also say, politically sensitive town as Royal

Windsor. Keep an eye on the museum bloke, he sounds a touch unpredictable. What did you get from him by the way?"

He looked at Abbi this time.

"Very little sir, except that he has somehow lost the paperwork relating to this particular packing case. He's getting a copy though."

Pawley accepted this quite well.

"Ok but look, whatever was in that packing case if it was stolen, could explain how this psycho, whoever he is, has been dispatching his victims. Start researching it right now. Try to make as many connections as you can between you on these events. Each of you needs to take up separate lines of enquiry. The answer may well be as you suggest Mr Dolby, in the ether somewhere. We've got to catch these wisps of smoke before they prove fatal again."

The two detectives took the Slough train from Reading and then the short line to Windsor, built by Queen Victoria for her own convenience for traveling up to London.

They walked down from Windsor Royal Shopping and out through King Edward Court Shopping Centre.

Zac looked up at the tops of the buildings, seeking inspiration. His uncle Samuel had sometimes taken him to buy an ice-cream sundae from the kiosk before the Saturday ballgame. On these occasions he passed on frequent small but enduring tips to the young Zac. *Listen Zachy, he'd said. Always look up at the tops of buildings. Those are the parts that haven't changed. The rest of the building's gonna change once in a while. First it's a barber then a few years down the line it's a laundry. But the tops of buildings, they stay the same.* Looking up now, Zac could see the truth of this wisdom as he caught sight of two sets – three and three – of beautiful wrought-iron Victorian lanterns, set high up in the red bricks of the tall building opposite Jungs Swiss Bakery. They were elegant and slender, with upward and downward facing points like large metal crystals, held to the building with brackets in the form of drawn long-bows. He looked over at Abbi.

"He's right about the ether, but it's the ether of the past."

Abbi smiled.

"Ok lieutenant, you take the past, I'll take the present and we'll meet in the future."

Abbi's light-hearted comment, heading back in the mild breeze to Windsor Police Station, contrasted with darker, grimmer thoughts. Nonetheless, for Zac they were thoughts accompanied by a sense of excitement – the thrill of the chase. This was becoming a contest of minds he thought to himself. Whoever this guy was out there, he must know the cops were onto him, and maybe what point they were at in the pursuit. Clearly they were a step or two behind him. This was a time for deep thought and recapping the events that had brought them to this point. They were at the Police Station.

Abbi touched his arm gently.

"See you not particularly soon then."

Zac nodded.

"Yeah, I figure this has gotta be a marathon research session."

"Can I speak with Lieutenant Dolby please?"

The woman standing on the customer side of the front desk at Windsor Police Station was not to be ignored. She had natural authority. The civilian desk clerk was quick to go back into the controlled area of the police-station to find out if Zac Dolby was in fact around. He was not.

"Can I take your name please?"

"Yes I'm Mrs McManus. Mr Dolby, the young American detective, came to see me at Eton College the other day. He asked me to be in touch if I had anything new to tell him. I think I do have something, so I need to speak to him as soon as possible."

The desk clerk made a note of the impressive woman's name and telephone number.

"I don't know where he is at present madam, but I'll try paging him for you if you wish. Can you wait?"

"No, I'm afraid I have duties back at Eton. I have the boys' teas to supervise. Please ask Mr Dolby to call me as soon as he can."

The desk clerk said she would. Mrs MacManus made a dignified exit.

Research kept the two police detectives busy late into the night. When Abbi got back to Ward Royal she saw nothing of her new partner. Eventually she yawned herself to sleep.

Chapter Twelve

Zac looked mentally and physically drained but nonetheless excited.

"Why're we meeting here Zac? And while we're on the subject, why so damned early in the morning?"

He didn't answer the slender green-eyed woman opposite him straight away.

"Stand there."

Abbi gave him a look but moved over to the far right side of the shopping centre.

"Right… the looped videotape captures everything straight up and down the mall right?"

"I guess."

"OK, so the shop door that was directly opposite the bird is this one here, the magic shop."

Abbi looked sceptical.

"That's what we'd call a joke shop really, lieutenant. Stink bombs, funny noses, itching powder…"

"Ok and joke shop, but forget the semantics. Look at the door."

Abbi looked at the large bi-fold door in silence for a second or two, without emotion.

"And…?"

"What's it made of?"

Abbi wasn't keen on quizzes and made a face.

Zac was impatient and eager.

"Mirror glass, DI Matilda! Mirror glass with no frame to it. Just two large mirrors in fact."

Abbi was unimpressed.

"And...?"

"No, it's really important. Look, what do you think will happen when you open the door out as far as you can?"

"Customers can go in?"

I'll ignore that wisecrack. Let me just show you."

"But it's locked Zac, it's locked. It won't be open for another three damn hours!"

"Ok sure it is, but look at this."

He pulled his tablet from his bag and started it up.

"If you were going to use that all the time, why did we need to meet here in Slough at this time of the morning?"

"Because we need to set the scene Abbi, to put things in context, right? We need detail, and we need to take in the significance of it all, as it happens."

The screen began to download and unfold a scene in Queensmere exactly as it was set out in front of them in reality. It homed-in on the joke shop and then, as if compelled to act by Zac's will alone, the bi-fold mirror-doors of the shop, in miniature, started to open. It was a slightly chilling moment, even on a small screen.

Zac looked with glistening eyes at his colleague.

"Now watch!"

"What?"

The view on Zac's tablet panned out away from the doors, capturing the geometrical arrangement of the flag stones of the mall.

Zac held the tablet up closer to her.

"Ok now look closely."

It was true that Abbi could just detect a split-second wobble. The speed was such that anything more was undetectable to the naked eye. And now the lurid and horrible scene of the slain swan appeared. There was no precise point of appearance that they could discern. It came literally from nowhere.

"How did you do that?"

115

Zac explained.

"Look when the mirror doors are open, the reflection is like an exact version of the mall facing the camera. Behind the supersized mirror-doors the swan could have been pulled out of the store, maybe attached to a quick-release wire. Then when the automatic doors close, hey presto the swan is left behind. It's sort of like when an ocean wave leaves a shell behind on the sand. The whole deal is real split-second stuff and that cranky old camera isn't up to the job. Anyway it's all in black and white and lousy quality. The only part it could nail was this kind of wobble."

Abbi didn't seem quite ready to accept this off-beat version of events.

"So you're saying that someone came here and sat in the joke shop waiting for the right moment to open the doors and then pull the bird out on a wire, behind the mirror-doors and then disappear from sight? If so where did the person pulling the wire, or whatever it was, go? Surely the video would have captured him?"

Zac was ready for this.

"No, not if the wire he was pulling was long enough to allow him to get out of range of the video camera and then at the right moment simply let go. This way the doors would have closed automatically. He could be way over on the other side of the mall behind that pillar or whatever."

Abbi looked long and hard at the shop and the screen. She then looked over at the pillar Zac was pointing out.

"Right so if that was how it was done, who did it and could he have acted alone?"

Zac thought.

"I don't know, but we need to ask Brydson more questions, maybe the security guy, and for that matter the mailman, Duncan Dewer."

Abbi nodded.

"OK, but let's mix it up a bit this time. I'll take Dewer and we can interview Brydson again together. This time we'll keep Wylie out of it."

Zac agreed, following up with a question.

"What did you discover in your research by the way?"

"Not nearly as much drama as you lieutenant, but I'll tell you about it on the train back to Windsor."

"Sure."

Zac paused. He let out a groan.

"Heck, no wait. It can't have gone like that."

Abbi looked exasperated.

So you did bring me here at this time of the morning for nothing! What's the problem now lieutenant?"

"Well the theory of the quick-release wire is OK for closing the doors. They just need to shut in a split second, giving us the wobble. But the opening part of the thing doesn't stack up. It would've needed more time."

"How come?"

"Well if you go through the process in your mind..."

Abbi glared.

"It's your process not mine. You go through it in *your* mind."

"Ok the pulling out part of the deal with the dead bird, even if it was already arranged sort of ready-to-go, would have taken more time."

"So it couldn't have happened as you had it?"

Zac looked bitter.

"No Goddammit! The swan, even on a wire, with all the weight and the whole bunch of mess, had gotta show up. It simply isn't possible to pull it off that quick."

They walked on for another twenty or thirty seconds in silence. Without warning, Abbi stopped short.

"No wait. Come on let's go back to the shop."

They retraced the hundred or so steps back to the joke shop. Zac was surprised.

"How come we're back here; I thought you didn't buy this story either?"

Abbi explained.

"Right, your objection is that it would have taken much longer to set up?"

"Right."

"Right. But the tape as we know runs for two and a half hours and then starts to over-record."

"Yeah, so what?"

Abbi went on with her line of thought.

"What if the doors were already open, and had been open for some time before they were allowed to close again automatically?"

Zac was tentative.

"Right…"

"So let's say the mirror-doors had been open for a longer time with the swan lying behind them, until the chosen moment then allowed them to close. That way the camera, if the swan scene had been set up in the previous recording period, would only show the wobble right? It wouldn't show the set-up part, because that would've been recorded over!"

Zac stared.

"Ok, but then the mall manager, the mailman and the security guard would have seen the whole deal, no?"

Abbi shook her head.

"Not necessarily. The centre manager Brydson says he got in to work at 5am. Then he did his early pass of the centre. The security guard passed through at dead on 6am. The postman and Brydson were seen just after 7am. Suppose the swan was pulled out immediately after this time and posed? It might have taken say just those two minutes, if the slain bird had already been prepped inside the shop beforehand. Then suppose that a minute or two later, the tape reaches the point where it starts to over-record? That would give the perpetrator time to just let the doors close, and bam, the scene is magically revealed at the *new* beginning of the videotape."

Zac continued staring straight ahead considering this information for a second or two.

"What did you say about the mailman? What time did he pass the mall manager?"

Abbi looked for her notes.

7.02 am. Then just after, Brydson gets the call from his wife, he says. Then he discovers the whole scene with the bird, while he is still on the phone to his wife. He's been standing with his back to it all up till then. He turns slowly, sees the bird, and is stunned. He calls his wife back and then soon after, one minute in fact, he calls the police. This call is recorded by the station at 7.10am. Brydson is then out of shot for some minutes. SOCO arrive at the mall at 7.20am. That leaves ten minutes unaccounted for, regarding his movements."

"Sure."

Abbi was unhappy however.

"Hang on a minute though, would it really have been possible for one person to both monitor the tape at the exact moment it started to over-record, and to quickly arrange for the bird to be pulled out into position so that it was discovered at exactly the right time, not a second sooner, not a second later? To me it sounds unlikely that one person could've done it all."

Zac nodded.

"Yes, I guess we'd better test the times on these guys again, see if someone goofs up. Thing is, some guy out there is guilty of pulling this stroke. We need to know who and even more to the point, why. Was it one guy, two, or more?"

Zac looked into the clever green eyes of his female colleague.

"You Brits really like to snarl things up. If this was the Bronx we'd be on some wholesome drive-by shooting job right now. None of this cobwebs and mystery stuff. It's murky, very very murky ma'am."

"We do it just to annoy you lieutenant! Come on let's get back to the train station. I'll tell what I've come up with."

They took the Slough to Windsor shuttle. Zac was getting quite fond of it.

"It's real cute this five minute choo choo train thing. Queen Vicky had a good idea there!"

Back at the Police Station Zac made a call to the number passed to him by the front-desk clerk.

"Hi Mrs MacManus. Something's come back to you I hear?"

"Yes Mr Dolby. I believe I've remembered something from before Tim was… well, you know?" Mrs McManus hesitated briefly with emotion in her voice. She was quick though to revert to her usual crisp voice, clipped and clear over the line.

"What is it that you wanted to tell me ma'am?"

Mrs MacManus, distinctly:

"I think I know who Tim may have collided with before he died, detective."

Zac became suddenly very alert and attentive.

"Really?"

"Yes. But look I don't consider this a matter for the telephone. Can we meet, Mr Dolby?"

"Sure. Will you come in to the station?"

"Actually I would rather we met elsewhere lieutenant. I feel rather concerned about passing on this information to be quite frank."

Zac was baffled by this statement, but knowing the character he was dealing with, decided to go along with her wishes.

"Maybe we can hook up in town?"

"Yes, in fact meet me at 3pm at The Chocolate Café please."

"Sure, of course Mrs…"

"Just on the Windsor side of Eton Bridge Mr Dolby, opposite Christopher Wren's Old House Hotel. 3 o'clock sharp."

The line clicked and she was gone.

Zac smiled to himself. These Brits sure were an oddball bunch.

The police canteen was busy and the coffee beginning its daily metamorphosis from fresh to stewed.

"Step on it Miss Matilda. I've got an interview with Mrs Mac in fifteen at some café joint in town."

"OK lieutenant. As I was telling you on the train back from Slough, it's a Pelican Argent."

"What is?"

120

"The big white bird Wylie thought was just another swan is actually the heraldic emblem of the Clan Stuart."

"OK right. What's the clan thing about?"

"Well, it was the clan or tribe if you prefer, that went on to form the House of Stuart. If you were paying attention the other day when I was giving you your history lesson, they were the ruling royal house in Scotland before the Act of Settlement. That Act of 1701 declared there were to be no further Catholics on the throne in the British Iles. So thereafter we had the Germanic House of Hanover, later renamed by George V as the more user-friendly House of Windsor. Remember?"

Zac stood up comically straight.

"Sure do ma'am."

Abbi looked pleased.

"OK, so the Pelican Argent is a powerful symbol of Scotland."

"Yeah and…?"

Zac intentionally came out with this cheekily Abbi-esque question.

"And Mr Dolby, as you yourself said, the whole of this case up to now has been riddled with history and mystery. Surely the other obvious theme, I don't know why no one has brought it up, is the jumbo-sized Scottish elephant in the room. It's been staring us in the face! I mean look at all the bloody Macs everywhere! MacManus, McCredie, Mac Brydson, McDonalds… See they're even taking over your part of the world!"

She was smirking but at the same time deadly serious.

Zac laughed.

"I can see you've gotten a little freaked out by this case Miss Matilda. Scottish elephants are like pink elephants and flying pigs, kind of rare."

Abbi laughed, but kept to her point.

"OK but Brydson is a Scottish name, so is Dewer the postman, Duncan Dewer!"

Zac smiled back, mock-enlightened.

"OK you're either nuts or you're onto something. Thing is right now I've got to see… who is it again?"

"Mrs *Mac*Manus!"

Abbi was triumphant.

"There you are! The Scots are already here in our midst seeking revenge for the Battle of the bloody Boyne!"

Zac dryly:

"Yeah, right. I reckon you could be seriously flipping out detective."

Abbi play-pushed him out of the station door.

"OK lieutenant, see you later."

Abbi was buried deep in work at her computer and surrounded by papers when Wylie sidled up to her. She didn't look up.

"Yes Wylie?"

"So has the Yank cracked it?"

Abbi adopted a bored tone, hoping she might remove the irritant at an early point in the exchange.

Abbi screwed up her small attractive face in mock-thought.

"Cracked it…um… no, nobody has *cracked it* yet. But if I can be permitted to get on with this research we stand a better chance of doing so, don't we? Aren't you supposed to have some big job to do yourself Wylie?"

"You think the Yank can solve this don't you? You know that getting involved with a fellow police officer is against the rules, don't you?"

"Don't you Wylie? Or have you selectively forgotten about us?"

"No, but that's all over."

"Yes, it's all over."

Wylie looked over to find confirmation in Abbi's eyes as well as in her tone. He changed tack.

"So did you know that Pawley wants us all back over in Reading later tonight?"

"Tonight?"

"Yes, an exceptional meeting, 7.30 for 8pm… dress formal. Don't be late."

Wylie smiled sourly and left.

He passed Amy Joss coming in.

"Hi Amy."

Amy smiled.

"Abbi, a message came in for you. You need to call some guy called Stuart. He didn't give a first name."

Abbi back:

"Sorry?"

"No first name, just Mr Stuart."

"But his first name is Stuart."   "No, definitely not, he said to call Mr Stuart from the Guildhall Museum."

Amy Joss left. Abbi looked thoughtful.

"So this is the Chocolate Café?"

"It is and thank you so much for coming Mr Dolby."

Mrs McManus again viewed the young American with a motherly eye.

"I have ordered you some chocolate cake Mr Dolby, I hope you don't mind?"

Zac blushed.

"Gee, how could I mind ma'am, that's really kind of you."

"Let's sit here, out of the draft. Will you have coffee detective?"

"Sure, black please."

Mrs MacManus summoned up a waitress-genie with one look. Zac marvelled at her natural authority and presence.

"Thanks again ma'am. Now please let me know what you've hit on?"

The woman looked around the café. For a split-second a look akin to fear came over her usually confident face.

"Shall we wait until they've brought the refreshments?"

Zac was puzzled, but deferred to her wishes. She did seem uncharacteristically nervous. Once the coffees and cakes had arrived though, Mrs MacManus appeared to relax.

"As I explained over the telephone, it's really not exactly new information that I'm in possession of. To be precise, it's information that sparked a memory and thus in a way new, but also not new. I am so sorry Mr Dolby, I'm wittering like a fool."

Zac was keen to reassure the refined Englishwoman in her distress.

"Ma'am really please don't be concerned, why don't you just run through what happened?"

"Yes of course. Yes you're right."

She smiled warmly at the alert-looking – she thought handsome – young man, not much more than a boy."

"The other day, the day after you came to Eton in fact, I was here in Windsor. I don't come over as often as I used to, but I was here at the library. I was here only because I wanted to return a cookery book. Eton's own library is much better I must tell you, but as one might expect, not so good for cookery books. I take an interest because of the boys' need for variety in their diet and pass on whatever small wisdom I can to the cooks. They produced a Moroccan dish the other day, Tagine it's called. Have you heard of it Mr Dolby?"

Zac said he had, and that New York had a wide range of foods from around the world. He wanted to allow the Englishwoman to relax but also steer her gently towards her news.

"Was it at the library that this new information came to light Mrs MacManus?"

She looked back at him as if coming out of a dream.

"Oh, yes of course, so sorry I'm wittering on again. It was the voice. Yes that was where I heard the voice."

Zac paid close attention to her words.

"The voice?"

"Yes, it was the voice that I recognised."

"And this voice that you recognised, who did it belong to, and why d'you feel it's important ma'am?"

Again Mrs McManus looked round the room and at the door to the cafe.

"Because lieutenant it was the voice of the man who ran in to Tim that day."

Zac spoke gently but needed clarity.

124

"But how come you know it was the same guy? I thought your husband was on his own when he ran into this guy?"

"Yes, but even then I think at the back of my mind I realised that it was the voice of a person known to me."

"How come?"

Well, you see when Tim first told me about the incident in Eton High Street, something started niggling at me. At the back of my mind I had a recollection of something from, oh I suppose about six months previously.

Zac waited for her to go on.

At that time Eton had been suffering from post going... well missing. One or two of the boys lost post, some of it with valuables inside, – although we repeatedly told them never to receive anything of value through the postal service. Anyway things started to go missing. Some giro-cheques were lost en-route to a number of other addresses in Eton High Street. After a time we, well it was Tim himself actually, notified the post-office. It turned out they investigated the matter, and eventually we heard that the man had been caught."

"Who was it ma'am?"

Mrs MacManus looked surprised.

"Why, a postman of course Mr Dolby, who else? Anyway Tim had been concerned that someone would lose their job over it all. Which is exactly what did happen, of course. I mean you can't have someone stealing post can you?"

"No surely not ma'am."

"Anyway the whole thing was forgotten and the man disappeared. The only thing we did hear was, that when he collected his cards at the main post-office in Peascod Street, he made quite a scene, saying he would be back to get that Sassenach of a housemaster. You see, that was the same man who insulted Tim."

"So this just kind of sprang back in to your mind suddenly?"

"No, not at all Mr Dolby, well not just like that. It was the fact that I heard him as I left the library. This is why I called you. The only thing is I didn't actually see him. I only heard his voice. You see there were two cars reversing out of the library car-park. Such a silly fuss they made of it I must say. By the time they'd cut off my view for over a minute, the man and his voice had disappeared."

"Do you recall the mailman they fired?"

"No, I never felt the need to find out."

"Sure, I see. But what then do you feel is the significance of this guy, Mrs MacManus?"

The handsome English gentlewoman again registered surprise.

"Because I think he may have something to do with Tim's death detective, that's the significance."

"OK I get you ma'am."

Zac felt momentarily overwhelmed by the implication, and from the intense attention of the woman of strong character sitting opposite him. He wanted to convey the fact that he was taking it all seriously, whilst remaining objective in his police duty.

"Ok I'll get right on it. Let me take this new lead back to HQ and see what light it could throw on the case. I'll keep you up with developments ma'am, for sure."

Mrs MacManus shone a brilliant motherly smile on the young American.

"I knew you would Mr Dolby. You're clearly a very clever young man with a bright future. Do you have a young lady in your life at the moment?"

Again Zac blushed.

"I guess I'm not sure ma'am, to be honest."

"You're not sure?"

She looked at him with approval.

"If you don't Mr Dolby, undoubtedly you soon will! I look forward to hearing back from you lieutenant. You've done well, exceedingly well."

She was gone before Zac could respond. He left the café feeling as if he'd been ambushed and his brain plundered, but couldn't really say why. He thought though, that this was what the other person should feel after a police interview, not the cop himself. Now for more research and then the evening debrief in Reading.

Chapter Thirteen

"Can you all sit down quickly please? I don't want this to drag on all night any more than you do."

George Pawley was showing his age. He looked tired and moved slowly. What he didn't look was beaten. The mark of this grey-haired battling police warrior was determination. He was no quitter, and this case wasn't going to beat him. He was nearing retirement, and it may be his last case. If it was, he would crack it. His growl of a voice was sounding out again.

"I want Detectives Matilda and Dolby, Wylie and our pathologist, John Courtenay, at the front please."

"John"

John Courtenay stood up. Abbi and Zac recognised him from Eton at the scene of the Tim MacManus murder. Pawley spoke.

"What have you got for us?"

"What I do have for you, after all, is some DNA. It wasn't obvious at first, and it wasn't noticed until we had the body of Mr MacManus back at the lab. The sample I have is hair. Only one single hair mind you, which we need to act on damned fast. It may prevent another killing."

"How long before we can start looking for a match, John?"

"As soon as your officers are out of here tonight, George."

The gathering buzzed with the news. Zac and Abbi looked at each other eagerly. If DNA was involved, things might speed up pretty quickly. Pawley hushed people up with a look, and summoned them to the front.

"OK you two, what have you got for us?"

Zac recounted the theory of mirrors and wires for the appearance of the swan to a mildly bemused gathering. It was received and digested. Nobody challenged him. It was left hanging until Pawley urged them to move on.

"OK Mr Dolby, we will leave that theory to develop with you. Keep us posted. There may be something in it. The event in Slough was so bizarre that I personally feel whatever happened there holds the key to this case. Now DI Matilda."

Abbi stood up to point to Pelican Argent motif and its Scottish connection.

"There seems to be an historical point being made here, but I don't want to jump to conclusions."

Some of the audience looked at the two young DI's as if they may be a bit of a circus act, pulling imaginary rabbits out of equally imaginary hats. Undeterred they continued with their report, Zac recounting his meeting with Mrs MacManus. Following this, Wylie stood up to go through the matter of the forthcoming re-interviewing of the centre manager Jimmy Brydson, the postman Duncan Dewer, and possibly the security guard, Ken Steen. He didn't say who would be taking which interview but Zac and Abbi made a mental note to put him straight on this as soon as possible.

Pawley was up again.

"OK get going on those interviews and into the bargain, do DNA tests on everyone and anyone connected with MacManus, no matter how remotely. Also, ask the post-office about the thieving postman and see if they know what happened to him."

Zac to Abbi:

"One for Wylie."

She nodded.

Pawley cast a sharp eye round the room, settling again on Zac and Abbi.

"Get back to the museum curator about the missing paperwork. That's well overdue!"

"Yes sir."

The eternally grey Chief Superintendent's head turned back to the whole room.

"This is a nasty case. Clearly as DI's Matilda and Dolby have indicated in their feedback, there is some kind of mystery here over and above the norm. There are indeed, as DI Matilda says, too many Macs! Why so much Scottish blood in this part of the world all of a sudden? When I was a young policeman, we had one Jock in the force and he was born in Wales!"

Laughter.

Pawley didn't look amused.

"Why are people dying? What's the swan thing for and how does this historical theme come in? We need answers please!"

Abbi nudged her American counterpart

"That guy at the museum's a Scot too."

"How's that?"

I said that guy at the museum is also a Scot. Amy said a man called Mr Stuart from Windsor Guildhall Museum had called. I still have to get back to him. Up till now I thought Stuart was his first name. That's how he was using it."

"So the same deal as the House of Stuart?"

"Yes, I'll go over to see him first thing tomorrow. You?"

"I'm off to research this House of Stuart. If I get stuck Amy reckons there's a specialist in family trees right here in Windsor."

Abbi looked thoughtful. That sounds interesting lieutenant.

Get on to it. Maybe those fresh American eyes of yours can spot something we've missed. Let me know how you get on."

Zac smiled.

"Sure will."

"You're here on your own DI Matilda. I hope I haven't scared your American friend away?"

Mr Stuart's voice echoed slightly. The Guildhall was still quiet so early in the day, and his eyes lit up at the idea of some conversation.

"Yes, I am, but no you wouldn't have scared Mr Dolby, he's quite unscareable."

"I must thank you for coming in to see me Detective Matilda. I do hope that I'm not wasting your time but I wanted to show you something. It's concerning the paperwork for that packing case. It's really very exciting."

"Good, what happened with the docket Mr Stuart? It is *Mr* Stuart isn't it?"

The curator looked faintly taken aback.

"Yes, Mr Stuart."

He moved on quickly giving the impression he'd prefer to gloss over the matter.

"If you look at this copy docket you'll see that actually, and this is the first time this has ever happened, the docket's signed by hand in pen."

Abbi leaned over to look.

"How do the dockets normally identify themselves then Mr Stuart?"

"Ah that's an interesting question detective. Normally they're computer generated. The name of the despatcher is shown clearly here in this column."

His fat forefinger indicted a column on the docket. He turned to stare with luminously round eyes at the petite woman detective.

He went on loudly.

"On this occasion however, the paperwork has a long-hand signature which could only have come from Her Majesty's private sorting office itself!"

Abbi stepped a pace or two away from the goggle-eyed curator who had been bearing down on her, she hoped merely in his zeal.

"How could that happen sir? Why would it happen?

"Now that I can't tell you miss. I have absolutely no idea."

"I'll have to take a copy of this Mr Stuart."

The curator looked hesitant.

"That's rather irregular, but of course if it's for the police. OK give me a minute please."

He managed with some difficulty to produce a grainy copy of the docket on an ancient copying machine.

"Will you need to see me again Miss Matilda?"

His voice suggested he'd like this to be the case.

"Possibly sir."

She held up the poor photocopy.

"And thank you for your help with this."

"Any time miss, any time. I enjoy it. Say hello to the Yank for me!"

Abbi half-turned, looking at him sharply. The curator was embarrassed.

"So sorry, I mean your American colleague. No disrespect intended I'm sure detective. We're all one people really aren't we? I mean the English and the Americans – even the Scottish?"

As she left Abbi felt strongly that something odd was at work behind the scenes in the ancient town of Windsor. She couldn't put her finger on it, but she was uneasy. It was her late father who had taught her to rely on her instinct. When he'd first learned she was going in to The Force he'd sat her down and given her his own potted guide to success. With a pang of regret she recalled that she hadn't listened very much. But he'd been right of course. Instinct wasn't the whole picture, but it certainly was an important part of it.

"Hi Abbi, I wasn't able to schedule the genealogist guy until later this afternoon, so that's still to come."

Abbi smothered a smile.

"So you got stuck right?"

Zac looked down.

"Kinda."

Changing the subject,

"Did you see the Fruitcake of the Guildhall?"

"Yes."

Abbi gave him an abridged version.

"Heck, that's going to be tricky right? I mean if we have to ask the castle about the trunk."

"Yes, it would be. Maybe we can send a representative of the Colonies?"

Zac grinned and mimed tugging his forelock.

"Yeah, we still see you guys as our natural masters, not to mention mistresses, ma'am. I'm sure you'd make a real cool mistress DI Matilda."

Zac grinned at his own innuendo.

Abbi smiled too saying nothing.

"So, you wanna come to the family tree specialist?"

Abbi, evening the score:

"Why not detective, maybe we'll discover that we're actually distant cousins. Wouldn't that be scary?"

It was her turn to laugh at her own witticism. Zac, for the shortest second, looked thoughtful.

Chapter Fourteen

As planned, their destination after lunch was the genealogist, a Mr Ely French. His small office was conveniently above the fishmonger, making family trees and Friday dinner a one-stop-shop.

"Let's get some smoked haddock Miss Matilda. I'll cook you dinner later."

Abbi was too surprised to object, so a minute later she simply rang Mr French's bell with several pieces of haddock in her handbag. After a number of coming-towards-the-door noises, they were let in by an ancient English gentlewoman with sensible brown shoes and a huge bosom. She suggested imperiously that I wait in the room marked "Waiting and Copying". In the said room was a genuine antique photocopier roughly the size of a small rhino and about as sharp. It sported vast extrusions of 1980's plastic cowling and arrays of shiny rivets and screws. The well-built gentlewoman came back in. Squeezing with difficulty between the copier and the water machine, she asked if they'd prefer tea or coffee.

Abbi chose tea, telling Zac it was the better choice in England because it couldn't be sabotaged without great determination. Once supplied with these hot drinks they settled down to wait in the "Waiting and Copying" facility. The room had all the standard features of a small-town professional office. In one corner was a dead pot plant. This, having expired about a year prior, was shrivelled but dignified in death, standing straight, brown and leafless. Along the walls were volumes of Family Records 1903-1975.

Ten minutes passed before they were re-joined by the sensibly dressed woman. She looked at nothing in particular as she issued her summons.

"Mr French will see you now."

They snaked their way up the narrow stairs to a smelly back room, into the presence of Mr French.

"Sit down please detectives. Now what can I do for you?"

Abbi started off.

"How far back can you go Mr French?"

The little man sat up straighter in his chair and straightened the lapels of a once stylish sports jacket. He looked keen to please.

"Are we talking about your own family history Miss Matilda?"

Abbi was simple in her reply.

"No, the House of Stuart."

The genealogist looked both surprised and amused at once.

"I see. Well that's not really my line. I mean the history of the Stuart line is very well documented, and very well known. I can lend you a book on them if you wish?"

Zac saw the need for further information.

"We do get that sir, but please stay with us while we give you the whole story. What we need to know is what would've happened to the modern descendants of the Stuart line? I mean the ones possibly still alive today?"

Mr French looked more interested.

"Well it's all a fascinating area of course. I mean there's an existing well-known theoretical claim in the Stuart line for the throne of Britain. That's from the Jacobites, so-called because their claim stems from James II. He was knocked off the throne because he was a Catholic. The chap I'm thinking of is Franz, Duke of Bavaria. He was the son of Albrecht, Duke of Bavaria and Countess Maria Von... um... blast... I do apologise, I forget for the moment. In any event he's childless."

"Is there anyone else Mr French?"

"Yes Miss Matilda. There's also Sophie Elisabeth Marie Gabrielle. Her family tree shows she's also part of the direct line of the House of Stuart. As recently as 2011 the Scottish Parliament debated repealing the 310-year-old legislation, which had precipitated the Jacobite Uprisings."

Zac was intrigued.

"So what happens if this Act of Settlement deal is scrapped? Wouldn't those guys then rule the roost?"

Ely French smiled sympathetically at the young American.

"It's unthinkable that even if it was ever abolished by Westminster, there'd be a challenge to the current House of Windsor, Mr Dolby. Now supposing the Act had never existed, then Sophie I suppose, would now be a Scottish princess-in-waiting to rule as Queen of all Britain."

Zac feeling he may be on to a new British dynasty looked almost breathless at this news. Mr French however was on hand to suppress this flight of fancy.

"But there's no way that would ever happen."

"Never?"

"Never, Mr Dolby. The House of Stuart's rule over Scotland, and the United Kingdom overall, ended with Queen Anne's death in 1714. She ruled from 1702 following the death of her brother-in-law, William of Orange, as joint monarch with her sister Mary. Anne condemned her father's faith, and the succession passed to Sophia, the Electress of Hanover and her Protestant heirs."

Zac asked, trying not to betray the fact that he was an upstart Yank detective, delving without schooling into hundreds of years of murky British history.

"So the Scots just sucked it up, right?"

Mr French considered.

"No not exactly. In retaliation for that legislation, the Scottish Parliament drafted something called the Act of Security, demanding their royal family continue with the next Scottish heirs. They tried to restore the Stuart dynasty. I'm referring here to the horribly bloody Jacobite Uprisings. These failed however, and the protestant line continued over the centuries to our current Queen Elizabeth II of Windsor."

Abbi was excited by the conversation and the intrigue of it all.

"So what if the Scots one day do finally get a referendum vote in favour of independent Scotland, Mr French?"

French again looked benevolent, pitying their youth and ignorance.

"I really can't think anyone seriously believes there would be a wholesale uprising, and a claim to the throne of Britain, do you miss Matilda?"

"I don't know sir, but then again I'm not an historian or a Scot!"

"You talk about this Sophie. I suppose she's the true heir for some Scots?"

"Yes lieutenant, for some I suppose."

Abbi looked over keenly.

"But just suppose for the sake of argument… there'd been a further child in the Stuart line of succession, another heir to the Jacobite throne?"

Mr French held up a hand.

"We really mustn't get carried away DI Matilda. Just because things happened a long time ago doesn't make it into some kind of board game with randomly movable pieces. There's no more Jacobite succession. You've probably heard of the Act of Settlement of 1701 I expect?"

"Yes but what if there'd been an illegitimate child, a girl or a boy, that's been simply hushed up? Didn't I hear that Henry VIII had a secret daughter who should've taken the throne in place of Elizabeth 1?"

Mr French was getting increasingly excited by the discussion.

"Now you're correct that there is some recent new research showing that an Elizabeth Tailboys was the Tudor monarch's illegitimate lovechild. She could have changed the course of English history if the king had acknowledged her as his at the time. By rights she should have taken the throne on the death of Queen Mary in 1558, making her the true

Elizabeth I and not Elizabeth the daughter of Anne Boleyn as it turned out."

"So it can happen?"

"Yes lieutenant, but it didn't happen, and in historical terms, that's all that matters. History is about what *did* happen not what *might* have happened detectives. It's rather like a crime is for the police I suppose. It's the one that done it that you need to arrest, not the ones that might have done it."

"So there's nothing you know of in the Stuart line that may have produced any unrecorded heirs, that may have survived to the present day?"

"No nobody else, Miss Matilda. Sorry if I'm the bearer of bad tidings."

He stopped and raised his head ever so slightly.

"Can you smell something odd in here by the way?"

He tilted his head on one side like an oddly oversized bird.

Abbi and Zac feigned not to notice. Abbi tried to hold her bag tighter at the opening, where the fish was now making its presence felt.

"So there's nothing fishy going on in the background, Mr French?"

Abbi kicked Zac under the desk.

"No Mr Dolby but look, if you want to do any research yourselves, can I suggest that you try the Eton College Library; they've an unrivalled range of volumes on the subject."

Zac thought inwardly that he'd go for a cake stop at Mrs MacManus's en-route to the library that afternoon, if she was at home.

Chapter Fifteen

"So what was your school like detective?"

Zac smiled at Abbi's question.

"Bronx County High School?"

"Yes, Bronx County High School. What was it like?"

Put on the spot, Zac had to make an effort to go back in his mind the five years or so just prior to graduation and starting work.

"I guess it was OK. I was the youngest of three brothers so I got the scoop on things ahead of time. I mean I knew stuff about the school and the other kids before I actually showed up there right?"

"Ok."

"So it helped me know who to avoid for one thing. And it gave me the low-down on how to play things. Who to sweet-talk and who the slime-balls were."

Abbi laughed out loud.

"It sounds like my kind of school. I was at a convent school for girls. They're the work of the devil, lieutenant, I advise you never to get caught in one overnight."

Zac laughed.

"I'll try hard to ensure it doesn't happen Miss Matilda."

They arrived at the master's house as they exchanged their banter. Now the mood sobered.

"Thanks so much for seeing us at such short notice Mrs MacManus."

"Not at all Mr Dolby. Is this a special friend of yours?"

She looked approvingly at Abbi.

Abbi put out a hand.

"I'm a detective too Mrs MacManus, really nice to meet you."

The gentlewoman clapped her hands together.

"Oh good! This young man here needs looking after, perhaps fattening up a little?"

Abbi grinned at Zac, who coloured for the nth time.

"Yes I'll work on it. He certainly likes your cake!"

Zac was keen to steer the conversation elsewhere.

"What we wonder ma'am, is if we can apply to do some research in the Eton College Library?"

"Research?"

"Sure, just like background stuff you know?"

Mrs MacManus looked wonderingly at the two young people before her.

"But surely you have computers for all that sort of thing these days?"

Zac explained.

"We do ma'am, but there are some areas of research where a library as old as Eton College's may wind up more useful."

Mrs MacManus repeated the word.

"Useful?"

Zac wondered if the shock and strain might have been catching up with the kindly widow. She didn't seem to be functioning as clear-headedly as on other occasions.

"Ma'am, should we maybe come back tomorrow?"

"No, no of course not. I'll walk you over to the library. Sorry I just felt faint for a moment. I'm fine now."

Abbi was concerned.

"Are you quite sure Mrs MacManus?"

"Yes my dear, the air will do me good."

They walked the short distance to the majestic hall of Eton College Library.

"Will you be OK to make your own way out?"

"Yes ma'am, of course and thank you for this."

139

"Oh by the way lieutenant, you do realise that nothing can be removed don't you?"

"Sure we do Mrs MacManus, we wouldn't dream of it."

The Englishwoman left.

"OK let's get started. This could take some time."

"It sure will DI Matilda, on account of it being a wild Stuart chase!"

Abbi pushed him gently towards the volumes for his attention.

"Get stuck in Mr Dolby. I'll only do dinner with you if you work for it."

Zac grinned, feeling inside a developing thrill at the idea of dinner with his attractive English colleague. He figured there may be rules in the Police Handbook about hooking up with a fellow female officer. His inner voice however argued that he was actually an American cop on secondment from the NYPD, so exempt right?

He leaned over to his oppo.

"Hey Abbi, d'you really figure that after all the eggheads there who must've been researching into the Stuarts, we're going to find anything new here?"

"Just get stuck in, Mr Dolby. If we don't find anything you're going to have to sing for your supper."

She grinned at him winningly.

Again Zac was inwardly thrilled at Abbi's cocky take on life. The delicate-looking English girl it seemed, was willing to do whatever it took to prove or disprove the facts. To her it didn't matter how deeply they may be buried in history. He found her defiance in the face of the odds deeply attractive.

"OK I'm on it."

Two and half hours later they looked over at each other cross-eyed and dusty with fruitless research.

"No supper for me then!"

Abbi pointed down at the accumulated books

"Another hour!"

An hour and a half later they looked over at each other again. Zac pleaded.

"Pub?"

"OK but here in Eton. I'm too thirsty to walk over to Windsor."

Zac looked relieved.

"Will the fish hold out?"

Abbi nodded.

"Yes it's cool in here, should be OK till we get it into the fridge."

They walked over to the Eton Wine Bar.

"What's next then ma'am?"

"I don't exactly know, but we can't give up. There must be a Scottish connection here somewhere. It needs uncovering before someone else ends up on the wrong end of another medieval instrument of torture."

Zac looked down at his notes.

"We're seeing the mall guy Brydson again tomorrow morning. Maybe that'll turn up some leads. He's gotta know something. If not why be so antsy for no reason?"

Abbi thought.

"He was pretty spooked by the whole experience. Maybe that explains it."

Her mobile interrupted the flow of conversation.

"Yes Wylie?"

Some minutes later she turned a glittering eye on Zac.

"So who d'you reckon the sacked postman was?"

The American looked blank.

"Mr James – Jimmy – Brydson, that's who!"

"So the mall guy does have something to hide?"

Abbi agreed.

"He certainly does, but how does it fit in with the case? Maybe he's just ashamed of his past and would rather not be questioned by the police. He must have a police record because of the mail thefts."

"It didn't stop him landing a pretty good gig in the mall."

"True. I'll look into his record before we talk to him tomorrow morning. OK let's get another quick round in. Then you can cook me that fish over at yours detective."

"Even though we didn't track anything down at the library?"

"Yes, you're lucky. I'm feeling kind tonight lieutenant. Let's prep for tomorrow over dinner."

Zac felt slightly disappointed at the idea of mixing the pleasure of being alone with Abbi with work. Nevertheless he smiled at her and went back to the bar.

Abbi, having spotted Zac coming into the police station, had a freshly brewed coffee ready for him at a canteen table.

"Listen Zac, sit down. I had a call from that genealogy guy French about an hour ago. I need to go over to see him after we see Brydson."

"How come? What did he say?"

"He said that he may have something for us, but that it's at the whacky end of the spectrum. I don't know what he means by that, but no doubt he'll explain later."

Zac was thoughtful.

"Why d'you reckon the museum guy played it shtum over his family name?"

Abbi studied her nails as she spoke.

"Yes I'm puzzled over that too. I wonder if all these Scottish guys know each other. I'm sure some of the ones from the main post-office and the sorting office do, but now there are others coming out of the woodwork."

Zac kept his eyes on Abbi's long feline scrutiny of her nails.

He spoke to her bowed head.

"Sure, it's like they're multiplying. That whole Scottish independence thing has shaken things up in these islands for good and all. You should follow the story Abbi. It's your history after all."

Finally Abbi broke away from her nails.

"Yes you were right when you said you see more as an outsider, lieutenant. It gives you a whole new take on things. I wonder if history is playing its hand in this as you believe. It's all a bit cloak and dagger for Windsor."

Zac shook his head.

"I disagree. I figure this is just the kind of joint where things like that would happen. There's so much that could come back to haunt this place. I figure the fairy-tale castle up there and its kingdom of bogymen must've seen some pretty scary stuff over the last nine hundred years right?"

Abbi laughed. Zac continued.

"By the way what's the deal with Wylie? I haven't seen him around lately."

"I think he's looking into the security guy, Mr Steen. Personally I think they'll get on well. There'll be no personality clashes since neither of them has one."

"Whoa, DI Matilda. You don't think you should be more charitable towards your fellow cop? He's a schmuck but he's still a colleague."

Abbi pouted.

"True. But I've got good reason not to trust him."

Zac resisted asking the inevitable question at this point. She would confide in him when she was ready, no doubt. Amy Joss put her head round the door to signal that Jimmy Brydson was waiting in an interview room for them.

Zac got up.

"Shall I pitch first ma'am or will you?"

"You start lieutenant. Maybe he likes baseball or another of those strange sports you Yanks follow."

They went through to the interview.

Abbi thought Brydson looked in a better mood than when she'd last seen him, but couldn't convey this subtlety to Zac while they were all eyeball to eyeball.

"Mr Brydson, Zac Dolby, pleased to meet you."

Brydson shook hands.

"You too. You're American right?"

"Yes sir, the Bronx New York."

Abbi smiled encouragingly at both men, as if to urge them to discuss something male and set up a good atmosphere for extracting information.

"We gotta be straight up with you Mr Brydson. We know that you were fired from the mail-service for the theft. D'you have any other convictions?"

Abbi revised her expectations of the matter of atmosphere.

Brydson was less ruffled by this opening than she had expected however.

"Yes that was a foolish action on my part, Mr Dolby and I do regret it. I've put it all behind me now. I suppose you'll also see from my police record that I've got no other convictions before or since that one?"

"Yes sir we see that. You were extremely lucky though in landing a good post in the shopping mall not long after your conviction. How did that turn up?"

"It was through an old mate of mine. We came down from Scotland together."

"Can we ask who that guy was Mr Brydson?"

"Yes of course, why not? It's Duncan Dewer. He does a round in Slough and heard about the job on the kind of postal grapevine."

Abbi looked up from making notes.

"Did Mr Dewer have some kind of influence then? I mean to say, knowing about the position is one thing, but then a candidate needs qualifications and the skills right?"

Brydson was placid at this.

"Yes that's so. I do have the qualifications Miss Matilda, from Edinburgh University, where I studied Business Management. My work as a postie was just until I had finished my post-grad through distance learning. It coincided with the opportunity in Slough. It all came together quite neatly really. The big mistake I made was getting desperate for money while I was working the Eton round. I was down to my last few pennies. I stole out of necessity. It was the worst mistake of my life. The only thing that still gets me is that they say I took more stuff than I did."

Abbi went on.

"Do you know anyone else from Scotland down here in this area Mr Brydson, apart from Mr Dewer?"

"Yes I do. Well… I did know Mr MacManus, the Eton housemaster. You probably knew that already though?"

Zac clicked.

"So you worked out he was the guy who told the cops about the mail theft sir?" Brydson's face didn't display any emotion.

"Yes I knew it was him."

Abbi cut in.

"So you had a pretty strong reason to dislike him?"

"I suppose I did Miss Matilda, but not strong enough to do away with him if that's what you mean."

Zac cut in.

"Why did you call him a Sassenach?"

The centre manager smiled readily.

"All the English are Sassenachs to us Mr Dolby. It's a friendly term you know?"

"Like Yank for an American?"

"Yes lieutenant that's pretty much it, a friendly term. After all, we all of us go back a long way together do we not?"

Abbi came back again.

"Did you collide with Mr MacManus in Eton High Street a short while before he was killed Mr Brydson?"

Brydson looked faintly taken aback at this question, but again kept his cool.

"Yes, since you mention it, I did quite literally bump into him that day. No harm was done though. I suppose I ruffled his feathers, that's all. He didn't even recognise me. I suppose he was too buried in all his theories about the course of English History."

Abbi looked more keenly at the man.

"Do you know much about history Mr Brydson?"

"Me? No Miss Matilda. My concern is ensuring a safe and smooth-running shopping experience. I don't have time for anything else."

Zac asked:

"D'you know Mrs McManus?"

"I know she's the wife of the dead housemaster, that's about it."

"We want to go back to the matter of the slaying of the Mute Swan, sir."

"Yes lieutenant, I don't mind at all so long as you understand that I have nothing new to add to what I've already said."

Zac signalled his understanding of this statement but continued.

"What we need to know sir is about your movements straight after passing Mr Duncan Dewer."

Brydson sighed, perhaps in exasperation. It was the first time in the interview that he seemed less than relaxed.

"We've been through this one several times now. I think I already said that I received a call from my wife."

Abbi's soft voice was the next one to speak.

"Remind us what you discussed Mr Brydson."

The centre manager had recomposed himself fully.

"She just called to ask if I could pick up some stuff for the kids' tea."

"What did you say Mr Brydson?"

"I said I'd get a pizza on my way home miss."

Abbi probed further.

"What time were you likely to get back sir?"

"I should've been able to get away at 6.30pm, something like that."

"What happens after you leave in the evening?"

He held Abbi's gaze as he answered her question.

"We've a stand-in for two hours until I can get back at about 8.30pm or 8.45pm. It isn't always the same person. Quite often it's someone I don't know."

Zac watched the man's face carefully as he posed his question.

"When did he arrive on that day sir?"

Brydson didn't betray any anger this time round.

"I didn't see him lieutenant. I'd been released in the early afternoon. My boss came down from London to take control. As you can imagine I wasn't in a fit state.

My mind was all too much of a blur by then. I suppose he turned up as usual. I was interviewed by a uniformed officer at home later on that same day. He informed me a DI Wylie would be in touch to set up an interview here at the station."

Zac and Abbi exchanged looks.

Abbi's turn again.

"Who else could've had access to the centre office?"

Brydson looked down thinking.

"I sometimes have visitors up there, but I'm always present. Dunc's been up in the office a few times. But he's a pal o' mine."

Zac pursued the subject.

"We know from the tape on the morning in question that you were out of shot for around ten minutes after your wife's call, and before calling the authorities sir?"

"Yes, I was trying to get a signal. The construction of the centre makes some areas a problem for mobiles."

"So where did you obtain a signal?"

"I was to the left hand side of the central aisle Mr Dolby, where the stairwell takes you up to the office."

"Is that where you normally work out of?"

"Yes."

Zac paused…

"Why didn't you go all the way up to your office to make the call though sir?"

Brydson looked irked by this question finally.

"It wasn't necessary. I wanted to act as fast as I could. Once I'd got the signal then I called."

Zac shuffled his papers crisply.

"Ok sir you're free to go. If we need you we'll be in touch."

Abbi looked over at Zac in disbelief. By the time she could gather her thoughts Bryson had exited.

"What the…"

"OK, OK, don't ask me, it just doesn't feel right."

"And for that reason lieutenant you cut short an interview without warning and let a suspect go?"

Abbi was genuinely angry.

"Is he a suspect though?"

"Yes, or at least he may be. Anyway how can we find out without pushing him? He was rattled about something. If you're just going to say 'sorry I nearly upset you, please go now,' how the hell are we going to get anywhere?"

Zac didn't really have an answer.

"It's just a gut thing."

"Well detective, as DI Wylie rightly said, we do the groundwork first. This is the groundwork! Anyway I'm going back to see French. I'll let you know how it goes."

Abbi left before he could respond.

Chapter Sixteen

Wylie sounded pleased with himself.

"So I'm off to Edinburgh now. Where's the fair Miss Matilda?"

"She's seeing the genealogist."

Wylie sensed a weakness.

"You sound a bit deflated Mr Dolby, lover's tiff?"

"Listen Wylie, I don't know what's bugging you but keep off my case right?"

Zac exited the police station. He needed time to gather his thoughts. Ever since arriving in the charming castle-town of Windsor he'd experienced a whole range of emotions. It was getting to him. Particularly vexing were the mysteries of British history and related issues of royal succession. These things were all intruding into the case and into his life in ways that were up to now unclear. Then there was this snide Wylie and the magnetic Abbi Matilda. What he longed for at this exact second was a seat at a ball game, a hotdog and a bottle of coke. He was aware at the same time though, offbeat as it was, that England was beginning to win him over. The oddball ways of the people, the smallness of everything and it had to be said, the history. History radiated from the cobblestone streets and each lop-sided building. His thoughts would probably have continued in this vein, had his eyes not been drawn down to his buzzing cell.

"Aw hi Mom, what's up? No I'm cool. No, Mom. Mom, the English don't even eat Baloney. Yeah, yeah right. What kinda pants? Boxers? Yeah OK, I'll let you now. Yeah sure I'll call, Mom. So long, Mom."

Despite his mood he smiled down at the cell as he put it in his pocket. It was good to hear his mother's voice, even if it was to nag him about his underwear. Zac could make out the flag at full-mast at the top of Windsor Castle's Round Tower. He mused that probably Her Majesty didn't get the third degree from her mother over her eating habits.

His cell rang again.

"Yeah? …… a longish pause….yeah?"

"Right, OK. Yes Wylie knows he's booked a ticket to Edinburgh already."

On the line Abbi's voice sounded less cross. She wanted to let him know they'd be meeting at the Windsor Nick with Pawley later on.

"Why's Pawley coming to Windsor? Did he say?"

"I don't know but see you there detective."

Abbi rang off. Zac felt relieved that she sounded less pissed.

His cell rang a third time.

"Yep?"

A man's voice this time. Zac listened for some minutes.

"OK Mr Brydson. I guess I could give you a minute before I head back to base. Where shall we meet?

"Sorry lieutenant but I'd rather speak just to you and not at a police station."

"That's not a problem Mr Brydson. What was it you wanted me to know?"

The centre manager seemed jumpy.

"The thing is I wanted to tell you that actually I left the shopping centre for a period of time on the day that the swan was killed, Mr Dolby."

"OK, go on…"

"I shouldn't have gone, but I got this weird call. I suppose you could say I was a bit scared by it."

"What was the call about sir?"

"My wife, Mr Dolby. You see working in the prison service she sometimes gets these threats. Ex-cons that get out and won't let go of what's happened to them. They blame everyone except themselves. You must get that in the police force I suppose?"

"Sometimes sir, but please go on."

"Anyway I got this call from someone, number withheld, while I was at work that morning. The guy on the line said I should go home straight away and check on the health of my wife and kids. I was bloody scared I can tell you."

"What time was this Mr Brydson?"

"I suppose I must've left at just after 6.00 am. I was back by... well just after 7.00 am.

"And your wife called you at what time?"

"I'm not exactly sure but just a few minutes later."

"So you weren't actually at the mall until approximately 7am Mr Brydson?"

"No that's right lieutenant."

"Who was minding the mall while you were away then?"

"That's the thing detective, nobody was there. I went there and back as quickly as possible but I had to hold on for a while. I was scared to death for my wife and kids."

Zac was sympathetic.

"OK so between roughly 6.00 am and 7.00 am, you weren't at the mall at all?"

"That's right. I'm worried that if it comes out I'll lose my job. That's why I've been so jumpy over it Mr Dolby. Sorry to have been such a pain, but it's difficult to start again down here. Does anyone have to know?"

"I don't know yet Mr Brydson, but you sure did the right thing by coming forward and telling me."

"Ok lieutenant, thanks for meeting me. I'll be back at the mall if I'm needed."

"Hi Abbi, how long have we got before we see Pawley?"

"Only a couple of minutes. How are you anyway?"

Zac smiled apologetically.

"Yeah I'm good. Listen I'm really sorry about earlier, I was stupid."

He pronounced this "*stoo*pid."

She mimicked him.

"True lieutenant, indeed you were *stoo*pid."

Abbi grinned, enjoying the moment perhaps more than she should.

"And he was away from the mall for all that time?"

"Yeah."

"But we don't know if it actually changes anything do we?"

Zac thought.

"I guess it depends on what happens down the road. What did that guy French say by the way?

"Yes French, it's really bizarre. He discovered this site on the web. It's the same one that Wylie has gone to Scotland to checkout. I'm not sure how Wylie will justify the trip. To me it looks like the work of deranged children."

"Why does French think its kosher then?"

Abbi frowned.

"I don't think he does. I reckon it all comes down to political correctness. It sounds as though he didn't want us to say that he'd misled us by not passing on all possible relevant information, however far-out. Here's the homepage of the site in hard-copy."

Zac unrolled a curled-up sheet of A4 paper.

He read out loud.

"The Jacobites' Return. Jeez what the hell's this?"

"That Mr Dolby, and there's no need to swear, is a group of nutters who still think that the House of Stuart should rule the British Iles."

"Yeah right! D'you buy that?"

He looked at the page in more depth.

"There's no address and no contact details of any other kind. So how's Wylie going to investigate these fruitcakes?"

Abbi laughed.

"Maybe he's planning a séance with the ghost of Bonny Prince Charlie."

Zac smiled at her hoping he was now fully back in favour. She added.

"No doubt he'll be back looking pretty stupid. He'd better have a good excuse for Pawley, that's all."

Zac checked out the time.

"Isn't it now we're meeting up with him?"

"Yes lieutenant, let's go. Pawley doesn't like to be kept waiting."

They walked over to the meeting room at Windsor Nick. It wasn't a large room and the Chief Superintendent looked even older and wearier in the confined space. John Bream the tech guy was also there. Pawley's voice sounded. It was like coarse sandpaper rubbing the chatter out at one stroke.

"Let's get straight down to it. John Bream first please."

John Bream again hurried up to the front as he had in Reading.

"With reference to the investigation and work conducted by detectives Matilda and Dolby, I want first to announce a change to one aspect of my earlier work on the tape."

Abbi and Zac focused in on this announcement.

"On the earlier examination of the rather poor quality videotape, it seemed to me that I couldn't establish an exact moment when the looped tape started to over-record. We knew that it could've been at any point after the two and a half hours was "up," so to speak. However when that moment occurred was entirely dependent on when the tape first started to record, which we didn't know. However since then I have been able to find out where the over-record mechanism cuts in. Without going into technical detail, I can now tell you that the over-recording on the morning in question started at 6.30 am. The tape then ran on until DI Wylie stopped it at 10am."

George Pawley got up.

"This means, DI Matilda and Lieutenant Dolby that we have a problem with the appearance of the dead bird, as far as your ambitious smoke and mirrors theory goes. In fact it would've been impossible to do, since we know that there were both a real live centre manager and a postman on the scene at around 7.00am. They would surely not have missed the scene in all its gory detail. So it's back to the drawing board on that one."

He dispatched an austere look in the direction of Zac and Abbi. They shifted uneasily in their seats. It wasn't the right moment to introduce the matter of Brydson's missing hour, Zac sensed. Not until he had other facts to back up an alternative theory."

Pawley continued.

"In another case-related development, DI Wylie is now in Scotland looking into the activities of a dubious group of nutters, who it seems may have a grudge against our own Queen and The Monarchy. Obviously we're obliged to take this seriously. Having looked at the background to it however, personally I believe we can discount it as the work of a bunch of loonies. This said, we need to do a good deal more work on this case. Given the new timeline for the Queensmere tape, we need to know if this affects anything regarding the movements of anyone that was on the scene at the time, and thus possibly part of some madcap plot. I leave this with DI's Matilda and Dolby. Further to this, we need more details on the historical aspect to this case. Some madman or madmen unknown are getting away with outrages that we should've put a stop to days ago. We still don't know how the bird got from Windsor to Slough, and we don't know why Slough is still of significance. Also SOCO have turned up this. Pawley held up another of the white cards that had become the trademark of the medieval style killer. Abbi ventured a question.

"What's on it, sir?

It's a picture of what appears to be a queen on it DI Matilda. Maybe with a history major at your fingertips you'll find out which one."

"Yes of course sir."

"Good, get on to it."

Pawley paced out of the room in silence.

John Bream moved over to Abbi and Zac.

"I've never seen him so worked up before. Retirement's coming up. Maybe it's a good thing."

He smiled ironically as he left.

"See you soon again, no doubt."

Zac turned to Abbi.

"Goddammit. I thought we were on a dead cert there."

"Dead Mr Dolby, just not a cert."

Pawley had left the building and now it was time to make good on his instructions.

Back to the grind, Mr D. I suggest a long session online."

They headed back to their desks and computers.

Zac was aware that his cell should not be ringing so early. It must be hours until work. He was groggy.

"Yeah?"

It was Abbi's voice on the line speaking urgently.

"Zac. Get over to Queen Victoria's Statue right now!"

"Sweet Jesus! What gives?"

"Zac just come!"

The young American got up silently and dressed quickly. Downing cold coffee from the previous day, he closed the door on his apartment. Queen Victoria's Statue is known to pretty much every visitor to Windsor. Keeping watch at the base of the short incline up to the castle's Main Gate. She looks down imperiously from her elevated plinth. Today untypically she was shrouded in white canvas and belted with 'Police Do Not Cross' tape. Locals, if they had been up at 4am in the morning, would have been intrigued.

"Morning Lieutenant Dolby."

"Hey John."

John Courtenay was the first to spot Zac, signalling to him with a sideways glance of his eyes in Abbi's direction, that she'd been affected by the scene. Zac could see she was pale.

He came up close to her.

"How's it going Abbi?"

"Hi. Yes I'm OK. It's all pretty horrible though."

"What happened here?"

"It's Brydson, he's been murdered, and not in a nice way."

"Jeez, Brydson?!"

Yes, it's another of the medieval devices."

"What kind?"

Abbi looked for a second as though she was going to throw up, but recovered herself.

"Take your time Abbi."

"No I'm OK now. It's a thing called a lead sprinkler. It's essentially a ladle on the end of a handle. The top half forms a kind of globe that can be removed, while the lower half is filled with boiling oil, pitch or tar. Nice stuff like that. The top half of the globe is full of holes like a colander. This is screwed back onto the bottom half. Then by shaking or flicking the sprinkler at the victim he's showered with the contents. He has to be pinned down first so he can't escape."

"Man! What did they use in this one?"

Abbi whispered back, as if whispering might help lessen the horror.

"Boiling oil, it must've been horrific. He'd had his mouth stuffed with rags and taped up. If he hadn't, the whole of Windsor would've heard him. Then he was finally leant up against the Victoria Statue and left to die slowly. When I arrived SOCO's were already on the scene. The pathologist has been at work for about half an hour."

John Courtenay came up at the mention of his name.

"Any forensics do you reckon John?"

"I don't know yet Zac. Give me a couple of hours to see what I can do. The body, as you can see, is in a pretty gruesome state. We need to get to some part of the flesh that isn't affected by the oil."

"Sure. By the way, do you know anything more about those DNA tests?"

John Courtenay looked surprised.

"I thought you would've been told by now. There's nothing to report. That single hair on the body of MacManus was from his wife, which is entirely normal, since obviously they lived together. So it's a no-result really."

Zac nodded.

"Sure."

"Anyway they ran the results through the central criminal database first. There's no match there, so then they checked against all those people who could possibly have come in to contact with the victim."

"Ok, got you."

Zac looked over at his pale looking oppo.

"I guess I may get Abbi away from the scene at some point soon. We need her fully functioning if we're gonna crack on with this case."

"Oh, there's one further thing Zac."

"OK right."

The pathologist went on. "It's just that we've now found out how the swan got to Slough. We found one of the post-office vans had a whole load of white features in the back. The animal must've been snatched from the river and then taken in the back of the van to Queensmere."

"Man, really?"

"Yes. Strange right? We still have to do some DNA on the van, but we're pretty sure that's how it was done."

"Thanks John, keep me in the loop right?"

"Will do. I hope Abbi will be OK."

"Thanks. I'll take care of her."

Zac started leading the way from the murder scene back to the police station. Abbi was still pale. She held something for him to see.

"Look here."

She placed a forensics bag with a further white card into his hands.

"It's a portrait of king this time. So, a queen and a king. All we need now lieutenant is the joker who keeps supplying them!"

She put the card in her pocket as they retreated from the scene.

"Come on, let's grab a coffee at the station Miss Matilda; I feel a bit nauseous."

Abbi looked over at him and smiled faintly.

"You're feeling sick? Nice try lieutenant. I'm not stupid you know, even if I am just a girl. But thanks, and yes let's do it."

Back at Windsor Police Station's canteen they caught the first brewed coffee of the day."

Abbi was feeling better. "The coffee's not too bad actually if you get it early. It's only after it's been stewing all day that it's undrinkable. It's not exactly Blue Mountain, but not bad."

Zac nodded.

"Like a lot of things, looking from a different angle helps a whole bunch. Take this thing with the looped videotape. It may seem that I took us on a wild swan chase there. But now we know that Brydson was away from the mall for an hour at the critical time, it puts a complete new spin on things. We just gotta work out what the new spin is."

Abbi drummed the table thinking out loud.

"That damned tape. You got me out of bed for that."

"Yeah I know. My apologies again for that."

Abbi paused to think.

"Wait a second. The tape was pretty poor wasn't it?"

"Yeah I guess. All the over-recording degrades the quality."

"So how much did any of us actually study in any detail, the black and white images of the people taking part in that little play on tape? What was really being acted out just before the appearance of the dead bird?"

Zac considered.

"Yeah Abbi, but we know that Brydson and Dewer and the mailman were there. We saw them pass each other and say hi, right?"

"Yes but we now know that Brydson wasn't there until after 7am.

Zac began to see what she was saying.

"But surely wasn't he back in time for the second pass of the mall? We thought we had him on the footage for that, right?"

Abbi stuck to her point.

"But was he, Zac? The way he described it to you, I don't see how he could've been there in the final few minutes of the video footage. What's more I don't see how it can be him doing the second pass of the mall, or him greeting the postman."

Zac whistled under his breath.

"Jesus you're right. Am I dumb or what? Brydson had only just arrived back at the scene a moment before he came across the slaughtered bird. He couldn't have done a second pass of the mall. He didn't want me to work it out in case it got back to his employers. Here am I sitting on my dumb ass with that information for hours without seeing it."

Abbi nodded vigorously.

"Right so come on. The tape needs examining again. This time specifically for the actors in this sick little drama."

The two continued to stare at each other silently for a few long seconds.

Abbi reacted first.

"I'll call Bream and tell him we're on our way."

"Message, Abbi."

"Who from?"

"That guy from the Guildhall Museum again. He says it's pretty urgent."

"Ok Amy, do me a favour. Zac and I have to go to Reading, can you tell Mr Stuart I'll be back in Windsor later and ask him to come in?"

Amy Joss grinned.

"OK but no detours detectives, come straight home!"

Abbi grinned friendly-sarcastically back.

Amy shouted after them.

"I almost forgot, Wylie says he's uncovered a threat to national security. I assume we ignore it right?"

"Right!"

Chapter Seventeen

John Bream was fine, having explained how it all worked, to leave Zac and Abbi to run through the tape of the shopping centre for as long as they wanted.

"Just sign it back in at the desk when you've finished."

Abbi held the door for him.

"Thanks John."

They settled down to go through the videotape for a third time. The grainy pictures started up and a series of boring and long nothing-happening sequences followed.

"It's not really Oscar material is it?"

"No lieutenant but stay focused."

Small indistinct figures appeared on the screen.

Zac looked at Abbi.

"So this is the second pass of the mall right?"

Abbi remained looking intently at the screen.

"Yes remember, because of the newly determined time of the over-recording, the first pass of the mall isn't captured on the tape."

Zac nodded absently as he directed his attention to the video.

"OK so that looks like Brydson in his baseball cap. It's a New York Yankees cap; I recall him seeing him wearing it last time he was here at the station. He's walking away from the camera. Man this isn't as open and shut as I figured."

Zac now bent in further towards the screen.

"Wait up. Is that the mailman who he passes, at just after 7am?"

"Yes why?"

Zac scoured the small indistinct figures.

"It's just the build of that guy looks a whole bunch smaller than the Mr Dewer I met."

Abbi turned to him.

"So only you have actually met Dewer out of all of us? That means nobody else was checking out a like-for-like ID, and you were distracted looking for the swan thing."

"True, like everyone else I guess."

"I know Zac. I'm not blaming you for missing it until now. But if that isn't Duncan Dewer, who the hell is it? And if, as we now know, Brydson was away until 7.06 am, who was it doing the second pass of the mall!?"

She started to gather things hurriedly together.

"Let's hand this tape in and get back to Windsor as soon as possible. Something feels wrong here. I feel danger, Zac. There may be more deaths unless we move it. I want to talk to Mr Stuart again."

They caught the train back to Windsor via the Slough shuttle.

Having walked from the train station to the Windsor Police Station foyer, they paused. Zac, who had been deep in thought, now broke the silence abruptly.

"The other thing Pawley wanted to know was how it all hooks up with Slough right?"

"Yes why?"

"So I'm going to look into that while you see this Fruitcake of the Museum again. Meet up for a drink later?"

"I don't know yet Mr Dolby, it all depends how many more nasty shocks I have to deal with today."

He looked disappointed.

She helped him out.

"Yes lieutenant, drinks later."

Mr Stuart appeared in the foyer. Abbi greeted him.

"You wanted to see me Mr Stuart?"

The museum curator was goggle-eyed with an emotion Abbi hadn't seen in him before.

"Are you OK?"

"Ahhh… yes Miss Matilda, Detective Matilda I mean. I seem to be more or less intact at present."

"So what's the problem?"

"The problem, yes the problem was and indeed still is the docket really. I can't seem to understand what happened to that docket. I'm usually quite sorted out with all my paperwork you know? Only with that one single docket, I'm having more trouble than with anything I can remember."

Abbi was calming towards the agitated curator.

"What matters Mr Stuart is simply if you've found out what happened to the original contents of the packing case. We need to know if there were, as we originally thought, medieval devices in the case or not. There's been another killing, did you know?"

The curator looked back at her with rounded, Abbi again thought, fearful eyes.

"Yes I know, and this's what I'm worried about. What if someone did tamper with the case, and now the contents are being used to murder people? Who'll be next?"

"Are you afraid for your own safety Mr Stuart?"

The man's eyes widened to an even larger goggle than before.

"Me?"

"Yes."

"I... well… I'm at the centre of the thing aren't I?"

"How do you mean Mr Stuart, at the centre?"

"I mean all of this plotting and murder. I'm… I mean… my name… well... I'm…"

He tailed off… He slumped white-faced to the ground.

"… Help! Can I have some help here please?!"

"What's the matter Abbi?"

Amy, get Zac or someone, this guy has just collapsed. I don't know if he's fainted or something worse."

The museum curator lay pale on the hardwood police-station floor while officers from other rooms ran in to assist. A young uniformed officer was first to arrive.

"Thanks guys."

"No problem DI Matilda. He's just fainted I reckon. Look, his colour's coming back now."

"Thanks Mark, can you hold on for a moment or two just in case?"

"Yes miss."

The curator began to move and groaned something about his head."

"OK Mr Stuart, you're OK. Don't talk for now. I'll call for a hot drink and we can take this up later today if you're well enough."

She left Amy Joss and the uniformed officer in charge and went in search of Zac.

By contrast Zac looked jubilant.

"I've got something."

Even the sharing of the news of the museum curator didn't appear to get properly through to him.

Abbi wanted to know.

"What're you so cocky about lieutenant?"

Zac crowed.

"Because I've found something major out about Slough. I figure I've come up with the goods on the swan and that other bird, what was it...?"

"The Pelican Argent."

Yes that. Like you said, it's the emblem of the Clan Stuart who later sat on the Stuart Throne."

"Yes Zac and...?"

"Anyway I googled it, and it came up with old records of George V. It was to do with when he "processed" from Slough to Windsor with his new queen. To "process" was like when important folk travelled around. This was 1911. Here, I printed this part off. It's from a newspaper called The Daily Graphic. There's a picture too."

Abbi studied the document.

Following the coronation of King George V on 22nd June 1911, nine days later the King and Queen, Mary of Teck, processed from Slough through Eton and on to Windsor (the Royal Progress) in an open landau. With them was Princess Mary, aged 14, looking towards the camera, and Prince George, aged 9. Here they are halted on Windsor Bridge on their way from Eton."

Zac helped out with the last paragraph.

"Then on the bridge they were addressed by a guy called Lord Desborough, before making their state entry to Windsor where the Royal Party was greeted by this Mayor Frederick Dyson etc., alongside other dignitaries next to Queen Vicky's Statue."

Abbi looked at him gravely.

"That it?"

Zac held up a hand.

"No. It also turns out the Latin on the second white card is actually the slogan of the Clan Stuart."

"Zac, shouldn't you have found that out from the start. When you first got the card?"

"I know, it's just that Amy was hanging around my desk at the exact time I was reading the second card. I just kind of asked her what it meant. She knew the meaning and I just left it at that. I guess its sloppy police work on my part."

"Let's leave that out of it for now Zac. More to the point I think I know what this means, or may mean."

Zac was eager.

"What?"

"However ludicrous this may seem, I think there's some person or persons out there who want to bring down the House of Windsor!"

"Jesus Christ!"

"Jesus Christ indeed detective. The emblem of the Pelican Argent, placed under the wing of the dead Mute Swan, tells me that the perpetrator is metaphorically slaying a strong symbol of the current monarch, Queen Elizabeth II of the House of Windsor. It says it's striking a blow for the defunct

Scottish House of Stuart. This, if you like, is the Jacobites' Return!"

Zac's tone was serious.

"So Wylie may have some real investigating to do after all?"

"He may; let's hope he's up to the job! I know its Wylie but I hope he doesn't get himself into difficulties. Come on, we need to talk to Mr Stuart again. Maybe he's got something of importance to tell us."

She got up, taking Zac in her zealous wake.

"If he's up to it, of course."

"We'll have to tread gently then Mr Dolby. That means *I* ask the questions."

They found the unfortunate curator with Amy Joss in a police waiting room, sitting up in an easy chair. Amy was possibly less fortunate at this juncture than her patient. Mr Stuart had recovered enough strength to bring Amy Joss up to date with the complete history of Windsor Guildhall Museum. She looked relieved to be replaced. She turned to Zac before going out.

"Zac, by the way John Courtenay called about the forensics, he seemed to think it was urgent. Can you get back in touch with him?"

"Yes, thanks Amy."

Zac headed off to make a call to the pathologist while Abbi gently returned to where she had left off with the museum curator.

"So Mr Stuart, perhaps we can go back to the matter of the packing case?"

"Yes DI Matilda. I'm so sorry about that performance of mine just now. I don't know what came over me."

"It's really OK sir, don't worry about that. Now, the case, Mr Stuart. Do you know anything more about the case?"

The curator paused and drew a breath.

"Yes Miss Matilda. I've been meaning to tell you this for a while now. The thing is I've been getting these phone calls."

Abbi waited silently for more.

"I've been getting some, I suppose, threatening calls about the packing case and er… also about my family origins, I suppose you'd call them."

"Please continue Mr Stuart."

"After your first visit with your American colleague, I received an anonymous call from someone, a man calling himself of all things, The Regent. Christ I thought it was just some nutcase. I still do of course, but it's been bothering me. Anyway the gist of the call was for me not to get involved with the police, and not to say anything more about the packing case. He said he also had to remind me that anyone bearing the name of Stuart, as I do, should be extremely careful in what they do and say."

Abbi interrupted.

"Do you have any idea who the caller could've been, Mr Stuart?"

"No, none. The number was withheld, but whoever it was had a pronounced Scottish accent, detective."

"And when was the last call made to you Mr Stuart?"

"The day before the death of that poor chap from Queensmere; Mr Brydson I think was his name."

Zac came in to the room and sat down quietly.

"OK Mr Stuart. If there're any further developments, and if you get any more calls, can you please contact me immediately?"

"Yes of course Miss Matilda. The thing is, do you think I am in any danger?"

His appearance to the two DI's seemed pleading, even fearful.

"Are you sure you are telling us everything sir?"

"I am lieutenant, but I fear something odd is at work in the town. It's all very disturbing."

Zac was sympathetic.

"Ok Mr Stuart but as my colleague says, just let us know if anything more happens. We're only a few minutes away."

"Thank you both. I do appreciate this intervention. Now I need to get that docket issue sorted out. None of this is good for the image of the Museum."

"Mr Stuart I wonder if I can just quickly show you some pictures to see if you know who they may be?"

"Well certainly you can Miss Matilda, after all you've just saved my life haven't you?"

Abbi produced the cards depicting two regal figures planted on the two most recent victims.

The curator laughed nervously.

"Where did you find these, detective, may I ask?"

"It's not important Mr Stuart. Do you know who they are is my question?"

"Yes, yes I do. Of course I do. The woman is Anne of Great Britain, the very last monarch of the House of Stuart."

"And the man?"

"Yes, that's Prince George of Denmark, her husband. That was a truly ill-fated coupling. She had seventeen pregnancies by him, and would you believe, not one of the babies survived? Thus no heirs to the Stuart throne. The next in line after that, because of the Act of Settlement, was George the First. He was a Hanoverian of course, and the rest as they say, is history. No further place in history for us Stuarts alas."

"Mr Stuart thanks for your help. You've been really kind. I hope you'll lie down when you get home. It must've been a nasty shock for you."

"No, no Miss Matilda, I'm pleased to be of assistance. Remember if you have any further historically based questions, I'm your man!"

They escorted the shaken but ever-talkative curator out.

Abbi was fired up.

"That tells me that somewhere out there, the perpetrator of these acts is driving home his message about the Stuart line. These cards say the Stuarts, stopped in their tracks by the events of history, are now on their way back. This is their continuation of the Jacobite Uprisings, and the Act of Settlement be damned!"

"Zac, are you even listening?"

Zac turned to Abbi. He was clearly excited and had been holding his feelings in while they processed the museum curator.

"Yes of course I am, but this is important. John Courtenay has come up with some results from the post-office van used to convey the swan to Slough, and they're really bizarre."

"In what way?"

"Well it shows a DNA match for two of the people interviewed and tested following the death of Timothy MacManus. One's a match for Duncan Dewer, the other is for MacManus."

Abbi looked baffled.

"OK so the post-office van would probably have had Dewer's DNA in it right? That would be normal since he's a postman?"

"No apparently not. That van wasn't available to Duncan Dewer, since he's not one of the mail company's elected drivers. Also there's no obvious reason why MacManus's DNA would be in the van."

Abbi stared at him blankly.

Chapter Eighteen

"Wylie?"

"Is that you Abbi?"

"Yes, why're you whispering?"

"I'm in a bloody dangerous position is why. I don't know who may be listening. Look I've managed to find out more about this secret society behind the Jacobites' Return website. It's all run from a semi on the outskirts of Edinburgh. I'm planning to go over there later this evening and check it out."

"Listen, for god's sake don't do anything stupid. You can get back-up from the local force. You shouldn't go in to any danger alone."

Wylie responded.

"You don't understand Abbi. I can't trust anyone up here. It's them and us don't you realise? The Scots are a different breed. I've found out you just can't predict how they'll react. All that stuff about Scottish independence has really got them going. It's all a bit anti-English up here at present."

"Listen Jamie, what're you ranting about?

"What? OK how about English-born school kids being bullied and ostracised by Scottish kids? That's what's happening Abbi. English family homes being vandalised and the owners attacked! Does that sound like a rant to you?"

"OK Jamie, just don't do anything until you hear back from me. I'm going straight to George Pawley for advice."

Wylie consented grudgingly.

"OK but don't leave it too long. This window won't last forever you know."

Abbi telephoned Zac.

"Where exactly are you at the moment?"

"I'm trying to suss out the deal with the trunk. It seems that the castle's private sorting office knows absolutely jack about it. They say they handled it at some stage because it's got the royal crest stamped on it. After dispatch to the mailman however, they've no other information. What's more, they don't recognise the signature on the docket. The mailman has to get a special pass into the precincts of the castle, then another pass to get in to the sorting office. I'm waiting to see if they know which mailman picked up that particular trunk."

Abbi cut in.

"Are we seeing Stuart again?"

"Yes I guess so. I think he still has something more to tell us, but he's scared. What about Wylie?"

"I think he may be in danger. Get back to me when you've finished with Stuart."

"Sure, but where?"

Abbi reviewed her scant knowledge of Windsor.

"Ok but it may be quite late by the time we've both finished. What'd you say to meeting up at The Firestation?"

"The Firestation? You wanna meet up in a fire truck ma'am?"

"No lieutenant, it's a bar, or at least an arts centre plus bar in St Leonard's Road. That's the long road that starts out life as Peascod Street. At the very top end is where Queen Victoria's statue stands. She pretty much looks down the route you need to take. Just follow her sceptre. It points out the way to go. That is if they've taken all the gruesome stuff away by now. Anyway if you get lost, just google it."

"Ok ma'am – catch you later."

It was about three hours since Zac and Abbi had parted to accomplish things in the matters of Stuart and Wylie. The

Firestation Bar was packed with pre-show drinkers. They were in to see a Burlesque show.

Zac spotted Abbi guarding two seats on the terrace of the popular venue, getting busy on one of the few warm early-evenings during a disappointing summer.

Abbi called him over.

"I'm waiting for Wylie to call. Any news from your end, lieutenant?"

Zac appeared more than ready for this invitation to speak.

"Yeah a real scoop. I went to see this guy Stuart again. He's still freaking out but he's got an awesome knowledge of history. He figures this whole Scottish independence thing's triggered a kind of lunatic fringe up there. Like you, he reckons they could be stoking up some nutcase scheme to restore the Stuart succession. He says they may be trying to unearth a bunch of little-known documents to take a pop at the Windsors. I know it sounds off the wall but he reckons there could be some real screwballs involved."

Abbi had been listening intently to this.

"And did he say anything about the packing case, Zac? I mean if there's still any device out there that someone has laid their hands on, these next few hours could still turn out to be deadly."

"He reckons Miss Turn, that's his sidekick, can't recall any mailman delivering that trunk to the Guildhall. They've a bunch of different ones. The only thing I can figure is that whoever has the trunk must have taken it from the castle sorting office and then swapped the contents before delivering them to the Guildhall Museum under a different cover. That is if it was delivered at all."

Abbi deliberated.

"We should speak to Duncan Dewer again. His DNA shouldn't have been in the back of that van but it was."

Zac looked across to see if she meant immediately, but was stopped short by Abbi's mobile.

"Yes Wylie?"

She held the phone tightly to her ear, before getting up to retreat from The Firestation's music. She seemed to take an age and Zac sipped his European beer appreciatively. You had to take your opportunities when you got them in police work.

"Wylie says he's managed to obtain documents from the house where these nutters, the so-called Jacobites' Return, are based. Apparently they all went out to celebrate the birthday of this Queen Anne of Great Britain. That's the Stuart Queen Mr Stuart mentioned."

"Is he safe?"

Abbi bestowed a brilliant smile upon him.

"Like you care lieutenant? Yes at the moment I think he is. But he says he has to scan the papers and then get them back in place before they're missed. As soon as they come through I say we get them over to French tout suite!

"Tout suite DI Matilda?

"Well he's French!"

Zac laughed.

They settled back for a while on incurably unstable chairs on The Firestation terrace and watched the passers-by. Abbi considered the facts.

"It makes you wonder, finding plots like this one still lurking about, centuries after the events that first triggered them. Here they are sponsoring death and dread in the 21st century. It's totally bizarre!"

Zac's thoughts differed.

"Yeah but like I said from the start Abbi, in this cranky old and history-riddled country of yours, some people never forget that stuff. Not when it's all about who they are and what they stand for. That stuff's in the DNA of the people and the place."

"Windsor's super loyal to The Queen and the Crown right?"

"Yes but we still have room in our nature for other people. We let you in after all Mr Dolby."

"I know and I'll always be grateful ma'am. But be damn sure there's still bad blood out there somewhere."

Abbi smiled at him.

"Ok but it'll have to wait till tomorrow. Another beer?"

"Does that mean we're leaving Wylie all on his own?"

"Well we can't exactly get all the way up to Edinburgh tonight, can we?"

"No I guess not. I don't feel good about it though."

Abbi looked to see if there was any levity to this comment. There wasn't. Zac was sound and professional. She was clear in her mind how much she'd grown to like this Yank.

They eventually parted ways at their respective apartment doors in Ward Royal.

"Don't wake me up at 3am in the morning again please."

"If I do it will be ever so gently lieutenant."

Abbi grinned, moved over closer and pecked him on the cheek."

"See you tomorrow Zac."

Zac retired to his apartment exhilarated. So sweet, this English girl!

French looked intently at the documents.

"This is absolutely amazing!"

Abbi needed more.

"But are they genuine, Mr French?"

"No they're complete and utter fakes. They are however absolutely amazing fakes. I've scarcely ever seen such talented work. If I didn't know they were fakes, I'd certainly think they were real."

"Isn't that a kind of a contradiction sir?"

"No Mr Dolby, it isn't a contradiction at all. The thing is there's no possibility, none whatsoever, that this practical-joke of an offshoot in the Stuart line, conjured up here, ever existed. However, unless you know this as I do, you'd be fooled by these documents, such is their quality. The reasons for their implausibility are many-fold and it would take a while to explain. But simply put, scholarship in this area of genealogy along with the accumulated research of many, many decades, refutes their authenticity beyond all doubt. What we have here is a breath-taking, fantastical concoction. As I say it's a huge practical joke! This secret society, what's it called? Oh yes, The Jacobites' Return that your colleague's investigating, must be having a good laugh over this hoax!"

"Can you tell us exactly what the documents seek to represent Mr French?"

"Yes, of course DI Matilda."

Mr Ely French settled himself deeper in his cracked leather chair. He was enjoying the meeting. He was clearly in his element.

"Looking here at the birth records, we have as I say, perfect but fake documents. They show the births in various towns, including Edinburgh and Glasgow, of six people. Here we have two unknowns, both born in Glasgow in 1966. The curious thing is that this record hasn't been finished off. In fact looking at this, I can see we have in front of us a fascinating if criminal work in progress. The names of these two in the line of succession have yet to be filled in. This is so exciting! It's like being part of a live misconstruction of history. It might have gone unnoticed had it not been brought to my attention here and now. Who knows what mischief this could cause if it fell in to the wrong hands! Now here's an actual Stuart, Mr Charles Stuart, born in Edinburgh in 1964."

Zac turned to Abbi.

"That explains a great deal about the fears of Mr Stuart at the Guildhall Museum. What else, Mr French?"

Mr French hardly heard the question.

"Looking further along this fictional offshoot of the Stuart blood-line, you'll see that Mr Brydson's here, as indeed is Mr McCredie, the other unfortunate man I believe. Now if we look at the most telling document, which is the order of succession, it seems that a Mr C. Stuart is actually in the top spot. It's all of no significance or importance of course, since it is all completely fake!"

The two young detectives saw things differently.

"Mr French, are you absolutely sure that Mr Stuart's the first in this bogus line of succession?"

"Yes look, it's all here Mr Dolby.

"Who else is in the line sir?"

"The next, that is 2nd in line, you've Mr Archibald McCredie, then 3rd in line Mr James Brydson, 4th Duncan Dewer. Then 5th and 6th we've these two blanks. It's really quite an amusing con. I've seen some forgeries in my time but this one is slap on the money. It must've taken great skill and a long time!"

Abbi got up hurriedly.

"We have to go now Mr French."

"Really? What a shame, I was going to tell you more."

"Please let us know by email if there's any further important information. We're really grateful."

"Ok Miss Matilda, I hope it's helped."

"It has. It certainly has."

Zac hurried to keep up.

"Where're we headed now?"

"Come on Zac for God's sake! It looks as though we've got to save Stuart, and by the looks of things Mrs MacManus may be in grave danger too. It could've been her husband on the list, perhaps with a brother or someone."

"But Mr and Mrs MacManus are as English as they come right? Anyways apart from the name I guess."

"Yes in principle, but don't you remember Mrs Mac said he was looking into his family tree in the in Eton College Library? Maybe there's more to it. She was only MacManus by marriage, but who knows what some nutter would think or do! It's just got to be this guy Dewer. He's got the whole thing set up so that when or if Scottish independence gets the green light, mad as it sounds, mad as it is, he can challenge for the Throne of Britain. We've got to get over to the Guildhall Museum as soon as possible."

Chapter Nineteen

"Mrs MacManus please."

"She's not in I'm afraid. Would you like to leave a message?"

"Sure. Can you say that Lieutenant Zac Dolby from Thames Valley Police called? It's real urgent she calls me back on my cell as soon as possible."

Abbi was a few paces ahead of him on her mobile.

"It's Wylie, he's OK. He says he's coming back on the next London train. Listen let's step on it to the Guildhall."

They walked faster without talking. The Guildhall Museum was quiet when they arrived. A mild looking woman in spectacles and sensible shoes was attending to paperwork at Mr Stuart's desk.

Abbi addressed the serious looking assistant.

"We're looking for Mr Stuart, madam?"

The spectacles on the assistant's nose slipped forward slightly. She pushed them back up with the deftness of much practice.

"He'll be in late today I understand."

Abbi focused on this.

"When you say you understand Miss Turn, what do you mean exactly?"

"Well I had a telephone call from a gentleman on his behalf saying that he'd been delayed and would arrive at work late today. I must say it is very exceptional for Mr Stuart. He never takes a day off sick and is rarely late in."

Abbi persisted.

"Did this man say who he was Miss Turn?"

"Yes he gave his name as a Mr Regent. Is there any problem with Mr Stuart? He's the nicest boss I've ever worked for. I know people find him a little eccentric but he's been kindness itself to me."

Zac reassured her.

"We don't know if there's anything to worry about ma'am, so best not to."

"Oh thank you both. I'll hold the fort until he gets in."

Abbi and Zac left walking fast, now concerned for the safety of the odd but apparently benign Mr Stuart.

Abbi reflected.

"Charles Stuart. Kind of spooky for him to bear that name, don't you think?"

Zac agreed.

"I guess so, now you point it out. What happened to the first Charles Stuart by the way? Wasn't he the one they call Bonnie Prince Charlie?"

"Yes Charles Edward Stuart, he tried to overthrow George 1st of England and damn nearly succeeded."

"So he'd be kind of a hero to the Scots right?"

"That's right. But if it's Dewer doing all this and he's already mad as a hatter, who knows how he sees things. Anyway if Stuart is in the fake line of succession above Dewer himself, I'd say he's in considerable danger. Probably at least one other person too, given the two blanks in the line of succession."

Zac became serious at Abbi's assessment. He stopped and turned towards her.

"So we need to track down Stuart right? I hope, what's more, we get the thumbs up from Mrs Mac soon. It really gets me to think she could be mixed up in all this. Besides if she croaks, where I am getting my next slice of cake?"

Abbi resisted the urge to say something rude.

"Focus lieutenant. Where does Stuart live? Have we got a home address for him?"

Zac checked his notes.

"Yeah he has something called a Grace and Favour apartment in the castle apparently. What does that mean exactly?"

"Grace and Favour is the name for privileged accommodation within the castle itself. It's usually for people attached to the Crown. I heard they've a Bookbinder to the Royal Library who gets a flat there for peanuts."

"A Royal Bookbinder! Man you guys are weird!"

Abbi laughed.

"Yes and we're proud of it. Stuart must have a flat there because of his job at the Guildhall. It also means we'll need a special pass to get in. Let me call Amy and see if she can arrange it."

Abbi paused to rescue her mobile from the bottomless lucky dip of items every woman needs in her handbag. At the same moment Zac answered his cell to a call.

"Hi Mrs MacManus? Gee thanks for calling back. How're you?

Mrs MacManus's clear voice could be heard asking why he was asking…

"Oh no real reason ma'am, we're just checking you're OK. I'll be over to see you shortly if you don't mind. I just need to make you aware of a couple of things."

More words buzzed back in a very English accent over Zac's cell.

"I guess in about an hour ma'am… OK sure see you then."

Abbi closed her conversation simultaneously with her colleague, pulling Zac by the arm.

"OK we're meeting at the castle gates as soon as Amy's able to get the paperwork done. She should have it sorted within half an hour, she reckons. What about Mrs Mac?"

"She's doing good. I can't believe she's handling it so well. All the stuff she's had to deal with. It's like only a week since she buried her old man."

Abbi gave him a friendly push.

"You're just after her cake Mr Dolby."

Zac took a moment to smile.

"Whatever I can get ma'am!"

Abbi, more seriously:

"Let's hurry it up Zac. The paperwork will soon be ready for us to go through security to Stuart's apartment."

Zac made a move.

"Sure. Let's scoot."

Abbi set off after him.

"I for one want to find out what's keeping Mr Stuart away from his treasured desk at the Guildhall Museum. I've a bad feeling about this"

They walked in silence most of the way to the ancient castle gates. The tension began to build in them.

"Amy's there now. Come on Zac."

Abbi and Zac caught up with Amy Joss.

They were all greeted by a serious-looking official figure.

"Sir, madam?"

The Castle Footguard of the Household Division looked a force to be reckoned with.

"Can I have a look at your papers please?"

Amy Joss passed over the documents in a rush.

"This should just take a minute. I need to check this with my commanding officer."

The three DI's waited tensely for the Castle Footguard to seek confirmation.

Zac turned to Amy Joss.

"Amy, do you mind checking in on Mrs MacManus for me? She's at this address in Eton. We figure she may be in some kind of danger."

"Ok Zac, if you can spare me I'll go now. I hope you don't get any nasty surprises on this one."

She looked over with meaning at Abbi and squeezed Zac's arm as she left.

Abbi had been keeping an eye out for the Castle Footguard.

"He's coming back now."

179

Zac shifted nervously.

"Right here we go."

They were led silently to Mr Stuart's small apartment in the Upper Ward of Windsor Castle, safely inside the confines of the castle's thick walls. Abbi pulled at Zac's jacket. She whispered,

"Surely nobody could have got at him in here?"

Zac shrugged.

The Castle Footguard stopped abruptly.

"If you don't mind detectives, I'll wait outside the door while you do what's necessary." They assured the heavy-set man that they would be as quick as possible.

A minute and a half passed for the Castle Footguard standing to attention outside the door.

Abbi led the way out.

"Nothing here. Sorry to have troubled you."

"It's no trouble detectives. Her Majesty is always keen to assist the forces of law and order."

He eventually released them outside the grey castle walls like a pair of freed prisoners from the dungeons of the ancient fortress. Zac's cell was buzzing again.

A sobbing female voice echoed through his cell phone against the high grey walls.

"Miss... can you slow down please...?"

Abbi's mobile now also started up.

Zac asked.

"Miss Turn? ...Are you still there?"

More sobbing...

"Listen Miss Turn, please stay where you are. I'm coming over right now."

Abbi came off her mobile too.

"Zac I'm going over to help Amy in Eton. Something's up. It seems Mrs MacManus has disappeared. Everyone's really frantic about it."

"Goddamn! OK you shoot over to Eton. Mrs MacManus may have disappeared, but I reckon our guy Stuart may've just shown up!"

They separated.

Zac got to the Guildhall Museum in advance of Abbi making her way on foot over Eton Bridge to the house of the unfortunate housemaster, Timothy McManus. Amy Joss was tied up talking with the housekeeper. Abbi was greeted at the door by a distraught Italian girl who launched into seamless speech without preamble.

It's very awful... Mrs MacManus... just she have vanished."

She pronounced the "ed" in "vanished" as an extra syllable. She looked wild-eyed. Abbi held her hand gently but firmly.

"What's your name?"

"My name it is Louisa".

"Ok Louisa, please try to stay calm. When did you last see Mrs MacManus? Try to think."

Louisa calmed down a little for the gently and firmly spoken policewoman.

"It is earlier this day... She get a call from someone. I think he is a man. Then she get angry. I never have seen her angry like this."

"Louisa, do you know who she may've been talking to?"

"No miss, I have not to know anything like this. As I tell you she is not angry like this ever. It is the reason why I am so worried."

Again the last "ed" was an extra syllable.

"Ok Louisa, please can you just stay here? If Mrs MacManus comes back or calls, can you let me know straight away? Here's my number."

The emotional Italian girl said she would. Abbi called Zac. There was no reply. She redialled, again nothing.

"Miss Turn ma'am, please try to calm down."

The mild-looking spinster was uncontrollable in her distress.

"I can't go down there again Mr Dolby, I just can't."

"Ok... sure... Miss Turn. I don't need you to go down there again. Just tell me more or less where he is."

Again Miss Turn's sobbing started up like a wailing machine. Zac waited a minute for her to get it all out. Cautiously he placed a sympathetic hand on the woman's arm.

"Miss... Miss Turn, I just need to take a look for myself. I don't want you to trouble yourself any more ma'am. It's for sure you don't have to go down there again."

"But what if you go down there and I'm left alone up here and he comes back?"

Miss Turn seemed to make more sense with the fear of desertion on her mind.

"Then you just stay here and stay calm. Nobody will come here now, not after what's happened."

The spinster looked happier at this.

"OK I'll lock myself in the office then. The thing is the only telephone is at the front desk. There's no instrument in the office."

Zac looked at her and decided that this was the most likely means of keeping her calm.

"Sure OK. Take your cell with you."

"I don't have a mobile phone Mr Dolby. I can't do with all that nonsense. People phoning each other just to say they're on the train and it gets in at 3.45pm. What's wrong with using the perfectly reliable train timetable?"

Zac needed to stem the flow.

"OK ma'am look, take my cell. I won't be long I promise."

He left the fearful Miss Turn in the small office, locked in from the inside, in possession of his cell. As soon as he had headed down to the underground storerooms he could hear it starting to ring. He thought it must be Abbi and cursed the fact that he couldn't answer it.

Zac looked in to the gloom and feared what lay ahead of him. He went back through what had brought him to this particularly unnerving moment in his young life. He concluded that it was all to do with being sent against his will to this stupid small country, with its murky past and its skeletons in every cupboard and every basement. He edged his way down the darkened corridor in the same direction they'd been taken by the curator a few days earlier, when checking out the contents of the trunk. The air was dank and the light, such as there was, came from bulbs that may well have been installed by Isaac Watt himself. They gave out a light that illuminated only the first foot and a half ahead of him into the gloom. They then promptly gave up like turning off a tap. He moved steadily on, knowing that he wouldn't be heard if anyone with a weapon was waiting for him in the darkness. Again he asked himself why he was here in this damned wet, cold country, down a hole in the ground waiting to be bumped off. These macabre thoughts added some measure of justification to his sharp gasp of shock when he came across the body of the odd but harmless museum curator. Into his mouth and forced down his throat, was a fiendish instrument with pointed prongs in segments like an orange. These had been expanded by force with a turn-screw to the maximum opening point. The net result was that the throat cavity had been fatally ripped open. Mr Stuart had met a cruel and unusual death. Zac leaned down and carefully withdrew a small white card slotted into the dead man's stiff fingers. This done, he scrambled his way rapidly back up to the surface. He surfaced into the main gallery area of Windsor Guildhall to the noise of Miss Turn screaming at the top of her lungs. Abbi was already there trying to calm her down and pointing to the key in the woman's hand and then to the lock of the door alternately. Miss Turn was too hysterical to pay attention. Zac, adrenaline pumping from his subterranean horror-show, saw it was time he took a hand. He surprised everyone including himself with the sheer volume of his voice. This and his fascinatingly unfamiliar tones suddenly broke the spell.

"Shut the hell up and use the goddam key! ...er... if you don't mind ma'am."

Miss Turn moved with surprising speed to execute his command and was out. She turned on Zac indignantly, completely over her fear and hysteria.

"Really, there's no need for that kind of language lieutenant!"

Abbi turned her face away, fearing her suppressed laughter would be taken badly. She grabbed Zac's arm and pulled him out of the building.

"Come on, we've got another damsel for you to rescue Mr Dolby."

"Where is Dewer?"

That question came from a weary sounding George Pawley.

"Why during virtually the whole of this investigation have we not been on his tail? Mr Dolby, you interviewed him."

"I know sir, but until the last few hours he wasn't really under suspicion. We've tried to track him down but it seems he's holed up some place. I was hoping to bring you up to date with the timeline of the swan's slaying sir."

"Wouldn't it be better to find the vulnerable woman who's gone missing? She may be in great danger. What d'you propose? DI Matilda?"

"Sir, we have as many officers on the case as can be spared. Also we've the main post-office in Peascod Street under surveillance. He should be spotted if he goes near any of his places of work."

George Pawley glared.

"Is it likely that he's going to stroll into one of his places of work Miss Matilda?"

The two young detectives were again nervous under the irritable eye of the old police warrior. Zac ventured back into the firing line.

"Sir, if I could just bring us fully up-to-speed on the thing with the swan, I'm real convinced it'll give us a clear motive for the killings. I figure it shows us why this guy Dewer could be real dangerous."

Pawley grunted.

"Make it quick."

"OK so the morning in question was August 26th when you asked us to attend the Slough incident. Now, after Abbi and me...

"I think you mean DI Matilda, Lieutenant Dolby?"

"Yes sir, my apologies. After DI Matilda and I looked into the matter of the swan's weird stage-trick appearance on the video, we got to scaring up theories. We visited a genealogist and researched the history. In the light of Duncan Dewer's suspected actions, we now have a theoretical time-line of the events for that morning. I figure it explains what really did happen."

"Good, get on with it detective. Perhaps the swan thing will give us motive before someone else dies."

"Yes sir. OK I'll put it up on the chalkboard."

Zac started to enter the sequence of events from the day of the dead swan:

26th August

4am: Mr Brydson gets up, makes breakfast for himself and his family. Eats his own breakfast, leaves the house at 4.45am and cycles to work.

5am: Gets to work in Slough Queensmere shopping mall. Has a quick coffee.

5.15-5.30am: Does his first pass of the mall. The video camera is facing from the south to the north end, recording face on as you walk down the mall. We don't have this first recording because the tape records over it, but I reckon it happened like he says. He checks the stores' doors on the right-hand side and goes out to check the High Street. He returns on the left-hand side, walking away from the camera and checks the stores' doors on the left-hand side.

6am: Ken Steen the mall security guard does his pass. This isn't witnessed first-hand by Brydson, who only checks by looking at the electronic log later in the day.

6.02am: Mr Brydson gets a hoax call from someone making a threat against his wife and kids, luring him back home."

Pawley's voice cut through the room.

"Just wait a blasted second Mr Dolby, what's all that about? What call? I know nothing of any hoax call."

"Sir yes, I apologise for not going into it before but can I just finish this?"

He took Pawley's silence as tacit agreement.

"Mr Brydson was lured away for approximately one hour from 6.02 until about 7am, fearing that his family were in mortal danger.

6.30am: This is the moment, I calculate, that the video camera starts to over-record. The recording period is two and a half hours. That's up to 9am.

6.30am: This is also the exact moment that we figure the wire holding the mirror-door is released, allowing the swan to be exposed to view. I'm sure now that the camera was been rigged by someone; my guess is Dewer on the previous day, having sussed out the admin office during visits with his buddy Brydson. I also reckon he represented himself as the stand-in manager at the mall. Either way, the rigged-up camera is set to over-record at 6.30am. This meant that by the time it's switched off, the staging of the animal is wiped but its discovery is not.

7.02am: Dewer disguised as the mall manager, passes an accomplice, dressed as a mailman. The figures weren't examined properly until recently, when DI Matilda and I looked at the tape again in greater detail. It's difficult to make out the exact ID's of the people, because the tape's such poor quality and the camera shots are at a distance. However we feel that Duncan Dewer can be seen, not as a mailman but in a baseball cap posing as Mr Brydson.

7.06am: James Brydson gets back to the mall in a panic.

7.07am: He gets a call from his wife.

7.08am: Brydson starts to turn towards the scene of the bird. Sees the bird and freaks out.

7.09am: He manages to call his wife back and tells her he's gonna call the cops.

7.10am: He calls the police.

7.10am – 7.20am: Brydson is out of shot of the camera.

7.20am: SOCO's arrive on the scene.

DI Wylie arrives later, and DI Matilda and I show up even later in the morning."

Pawley looked over.

"What was Brydson doing in the missing ten minutes detective?"

"We think that he panicked. Maybe he figured the office was being turned over or something and he'd lose his job. That's why he's out of shot."

To add to this sir, I now feel sure that Duncan Dewer is part of this crazy Jacobites' Return outfit. He's low down in the fake line of succession, giving him a good reason to rid himself of those higher up, namely Mr MacManus, Mr McCredie, Mr Brydson and Mr Stuart. The fact is that Dewer had means, motive and opportunity sir."

"Ok Mr Dolby and now we have to act. We've someone, maybe more than one, in grave danger. It's what we do from now on that matters most!"

"Yes sir. We're going out right now ourselves, to up the ante. I hope we can get the jump on Dewer from now on."

"Very good detective, very good. Just make sure it doesn't involve crystal balls or smoke and mirrors! And I'll still require an explanation of why I wasn't informed about Mr Brydson's absence from the shopping arcade."

Pawley grunted as he walked out.

Zac sighed.

"Man, what now?"

Abbi looked across at her American oppo.

"What is it that Dewer wants? If we can think of that, we can probably guess where he's headed and what he plans to do."

Zac responded by holding out his hand.

"Take a look Abbi."

He passed her the white card he had recovered from the body of Mr Stuart.

Abbi looked baffled.

"Mary Queen of Scots?"

"Yeah even I get that. But what can it mean except that he's looking to take up the crown where she left off?"

Abbi bit her lip.

"It'll be bloody if push comes to shove. What I don't understand is why her picture? We'll have to leave it for now.

There's too much going on to dwell on it. What would Dewer's next move be, and why would he have anything against Mrs Mac?"

Before he could answer Zac's cell went.

"Hi Mr French? Hi, can I help you?"

Zac went very quiet for a few long minutes.

"Sure I see, I see. Thank you sir, thanks. OK so long."

"What?"

"You'll never believe this."

"What!"

This guy French has been doing some real clever sleuthing on his own account. He's come up with the missing names in the fake Stuart line."

"How?"

He noticed that the fake papers had been over-written, leaving just enough of a faint impression for him to make out what's on the draft version of the off-shoot family tree. It wasn't completed by the forger, but the names were readable under strong light."

"And?"

"It's the MacManuses."

"What?!"

"You seem to be stuck in one-word expletive mode Miss Matilda."

"What?"

"You're doing it again."

Abbi changed tack.

"Ok that's what we thought it may be right? That doesn't change anything does it?"

"Yes but that's not all. It turns out the Macs weren't husband and wife. They're in fact brother and sister. Brother and sister, and more to the point, twins!"

"Twins!?"

"Yes Abbi, twins. You know like when two kids come out looking the same?"

Abbi ignored this, stepping up a gear.

"Hell! We need to get onto John Courtenay about this. Maybe he can help unravel it. It's all getting messy."

"The DNA we found on the body of Mr Timothy MacManus, the hair that is, contained the same DNA as we found in the van, and thus matches Mrs MacManus too."

"Yes John but how can it be that a long hair, clearly a woman's hair, has the exact same DNA as Mr MacManus? His sister may have been a twin but she's also a woman. They can't have identical DNA right?"

John Courtenay seemed intrigued by the question.

Actually ordinarily you'd be right Abbi. Generally the answer is no. Identical, what we call monozygotic twins, are always the same gender because they come from a single zygote. That's a kind of double-yoked egg. This contains either male XY or female XX sex chromosomes. However, there are a few rare cases of mutation. In these strange cases male twins, if one twin loses the Y chromosome, develop as females. It's called Turner Syndrome. The individual is always short of stature and lacks ovarian development. It's extremely rare but it can occur."

"So if Mrs MacManus is one of those, she's probably in even more danger, being in the line of succession right? But wait, no. She's a woman and can't sit on the throne can she?"

Zac intervened.

"That was the deal Abbi. But I believe in 2013 the law on female succession changed. So if you put her in this fantasy Stuart line she does have a logical claim, even if it's a complete scam. Like Pawley says we need to find Dewer right now!"

Chapter Twenty

There was a buzz of excitement and anxiety. Police searchlights fanned out over the dark edges of the Long Walk. What do we know Amy?"

"Nothing much Abbi. An off-duty officer reported seeing a man and a woman at the castle gates at the top of the Long Walk. That's why we're here."

Zac was deep in thought until Abbi delivered an elbow to his ribs.

"What's up lieutenant?"

Zac locked eyes with her.

"I can't see how Dewer got into the Guildhall. There was no sighting of him going in and Miss Turn was there all the time. He didn't go past her, that's for sure or she'd have told us. And she'd have been like a zillion times more hysterical than she was."

"So what are you thinking?"

"I don't know, it's just weird that's all. If he didn't pass anyone, how did he get in to murder Charles Stuart?"

Amy Joss who had been keeping pace with them, stopped in her tracks.

"The tunnels!"

Zac and Abbi halted at this statement too. Abbi's voice came across hoarsely in the damp air.

"Tunnels?"

"Yes, or passages if you prefer."

Abbi didn't seem to prefer, looking across aghast.

"What are you saying Amy? That there're secret passages under the Guildhall?"

"Yes Abbi. Apparently they come all the way from Windsor Castle itself to the top of the Long Walk, with a tangent off at the Guildhall. Supposedly they were all bricked up years ago though."

"I'm going back."

Both women turned on Zac as if he was mad. Abbi was first to react.

"The hell you are!"

"No I am. Look you and Amy go on ahead with uniform. If there's a possibility that Mrs Mac is being held by this crazy guy, someone's got to cover that angle right?"

Abbi appealed for support.

"Amy tell him!"

"Abbi, maybe Zac's right. After all you wouldn't want to be alone with an utter nutter would you?"

"I've been stuck with this nutter plenty."

She pushed Zac away half-angry half-upset.

"OK go! But get back alive Mr Dolby. There's no way I'm shipping your stupid corpse back to The States."

The emotion in her voice made it evident how important her partner in crime had become to her. Zac put a reassuring arm round her shoulder.

"Ma'am we'll soon be eating Mrs Mac's cake and joshing over this."

Abbi said she didn't think so. Zac smiled a goodbye and turned back. He was instantly and absolutely absorbed into the gloom.

"I hope he doesn't do anything bloody stupid Amy."

Her colleague took her arm.

"Come on Abbi. He knows how to look after himself. Look he's nearly learned the language already. He'll soon be as English as you and me."

"You and *I* Amy, you and *I*."

They laughed despite themselves probing forward into the darkness to join the main party.

Zac was back at the Guildhall Museum not long after Abbi and Amy had been laughing over the niceties of the English language. He began to regret his block-headed moment of bravado by the time he found himself in the yellow half-light of the storage rooms in the underbelly of the old building. He traced the same narrow and damp corridors as on the two previous occasions he'd visited that place, avoiding with a shudder the spot where Mr Charles Stuart had met his lurid end. Some five minutes of following his nose rather than any specific information, got Zac to the end of the supply of electric light. There was nothing for it but to turn back. He dialled Abbi to see what was going on in the over-ground world.

"Shit!"

If there had been any chance of a signal Abbi would've told him that there was no change at her end. As it was, Zac used his cell phone's light to peer further in to the gloom. If he hadn't tried to call Abbi he wouldn't have turned on his cell. If he hadn't turned on his cell he wouldn't have seen, in the meagre extra light it gave out, a pile of newly disturbed bricks revealing a dark void from the corridor to god knows where. Either way, this is how life works and Zac stepped over the bricks and into the unknown. Following a tunnel that had been excavated hundreds of years before, Zac made his earthworm's progress from the Guildhall towards the Long Walk. He was in fact making his subterranean way slowly in the direction of his police colleagues.

"Where's that idiot Yank?"

Amy Joss put out a reassuring hand.

"Stay calm Abbi. He'll be fine."

"Amy you're local, where are we actually going?"

"This way is to the Copper Horse. We used to come here for picnics when I was a kid. The horse is a bronze statue of George III on his charger. It's really impressive.

"Right let's go and see if George has company."

"DI Matilda?"

"Yes?"

A young uniformed officer bounded up to the two women.

"We understand that the earlier sighting of a couple was incorrect miss. The latest is that a lone female may be somewhere up near the horse, but we can't be sure." "Ok thanks."

"What's some random woman doing out here at this time of night on her own? She could be in real danger."

Amy couldn't think of a reason.

"Let's call Zac for Christ's sake."

"If he's in the basement of the Guildhall Abbi, he won't have a signal for sure."

Abbi tried anyway, only to prove Amy right.

"Shit! OK let's catch up with the rest Amy. We should be at the front if something kicks off."

The two young women quickened their pace until they arrived at a group of uniformed and plain-clothes officers fairly close to the Copper Horse. Some meters away from the statue, their impromptu pools of light from torches and mobile phones afforded some but very little light.

Abbi called out.

"Can we get some more light on to the statue please?"

A further young police constable hurried up in response.

"We need to get a lot closer to do that miss, but noises were heard coming from the other side of the statue, so we've been asked to hold off for a minute to see what happens."

Abbi nodded.

"Ok we'll give it a minute."

"Goddammit! These Brits really are nuts!"

Zac's progress had taken him along some dank and difficult snake-like tunnels, seen now for the first time he guessed by an upstart Yank. What he hadn't bargained for was the next dead body. He shone his torch hesitantly at the curled up body of a slimly-built man in his early fifties. He was wearing clothes slightly too young for a man of his age. Zac recognised him immediately as the mailman Duncan Dewer. Unlike the roll-call of gruesome victims that preceded him, Mr Dewer had been dispatched as far as Zac could make out, by a single slash to the neck. The time for a close examination of Duncan Dewer was not now, Zac guessed. Right now he faced the choice to either go forward to seek an exit somewhere unknown, or to turn back and re-join Abbi and the others. He opted finally to turn back, fearing that this new puzzle of the dead suspect may well portend something very worrying indeed. Whoever was behind this killing and all the killings was obviously a deadly killer and a madman. There was no time to lose. He turned back, nearly falling over something hard and square. The hiding place for the illusive trunk was a good one he had to admit. Having peered briefly inside, Zac realised that the missing trunk had a number of grim secrets still to pass on. The moment for this was also later he concluded. Now it was time to get back to Abbi.

Amy sounded strained.

"Abbi, what should we do?"

"Not sure. I'll try Zac again."

Thirty seconds passed.

"No, still nothing."

Another uniformed officer came up

"Nothing's been heard for over two minutes miss."

"Amy I'm going to move round to the other side of The Copper Horse. I want you to stay a few feet behind me."

Amy Joss didn't like the idea but for Abbi, this was clearly a decision not a suggestion. They informed the main group of officers of the plan and started to creep silently towards the back of the statue. Close up it was a really impressive statue, and in the faint eerie light from many small sources, ghostly and menacing.

"Stay behind me Amy, I don't want more than one of us in harm's way."

The two women inched forward. The weak light of the torches began to be obscured by the large statue, and Abbi's shadow elongated strangely on the ground as she moved. There was complete silence. She was halfway round the huge figure of George III and steeling herself to go on. She reflected that it was easily the hardest thing she'd had to do during her time in the force. The dirty streets of Manchester seemed suddenly appealing to her; drunken teenagers, Friday night brawls. It all seemed suddenly a lot more wholesome than this bizarre game of hide and seek... A minute passed as she continued to edge round the huge metal statue...

"Abbi!!"

Amy Joss's high-pitched scream pierced the air.

A man's voice rang out.

"Abbi!! Christ what's happening?!"

Zac, having retraced his way back to the usual exit of the Guildhall, had hitched a lift in a park-warden's car. He ran up breathless and wild-eyed.

"What's happened?! Amy! What's happened to Abbi!?"

Amy Joss was sobbing. The rest of the police group had assembled, deeply shocked, in total silence at the spot.

One of the plain-clothes officers came to Zac's side speaking softly.

"What's that sir?"

Looking up in the half-light they made out the figures of three large white birds.

"That, constable, is the emblem of the Clan Stuart."

Alongside the flapping banner of the three white birds that Zac now knew to be Pelican Argents, was the woman Zac had once known as Mrs McManus. She was a woman utterly transformed. The light of madness shone in her eyes. She stood upright in the style of a pint-sized Amazonian warrior, holding Abbi's slim, delicate arm in an iron grip. She was on a self-styled plinth holding a knife, bloody from recently slitting the throat of her once loyal accomplice, Duncan Dewer. Zac moved into the cold light around the crazed woman.

His clear American tones added a curious quality to the very English scene.

"Mary Queen of Scots I presume? You first name is Mary isn't it Mrs MacManus?"

He almost cooed at the woman.

She deigned to look his way.

Zac spoke again.

"Why Mr Dewer ma'am?"

The woman who had been the dignified Mrs MacManus sneered at the young American.

"Why should I waste my breath on you Lieutenant Dolby? You, from a country that doesn't begin to understand history, has precious little of it, coming over here to question me?"

"Yes I know I am just a Yank. Sorry about that ma'am. Let me ask you again though, why Mr Dewer?"

Mrs MacManus spat out her words.

"Because detective, he'd served his purpose. The laws on succession are now in my favour. I… (louder) I am the true successor to the Crown of Britain. It's my obligation and my privilege to carry forward the noble future of Scotland. The Scots are finally rising up to free themselves from the yoke of the English forever. I shall take the throne. It's my birth-right."

She screamed the words down at her audience from her makeshift dais, throwing back her head wildly.

"But you, Mrs MacManus, are no more entitled than I am. You've no royal blood in your veins at all. This is all fiction."

He pointed to the plinth and the banner.

"This is the work of a forger. You're as English as tea and cake!"

She screamed back in anger.

"Nonsense! When you came to Eton College Library I thought even dimwits like you two detectives would accidently stumble on our true lineage. My brother and I go back to the Battle of the Boyne. We fought against the accursed English. Our family died horrible deaths."

"Yes ma'am but you don't go back in the royal bloodline. You're not a Stuart, you're a commoner."

The apparition on her dais screamed in fury again.

"I took on the job. I have the right. I engaged my regent to do my work. At my bidding he helped to rid the new realm of various usurpers and traitors. Dewer was my servant. I'm the Queen. Without him I can now take the throne for myself. All the extras in the historic drama have now been eliminated, fools that they were."

Zac came back.

"Dewer killed for you, moved the swan for you. Not only that, he rigged the mall tape and got Brydson out of the way for your charade in the mall to work."

The self-styled monarch laughed shrilly.

"Yes a neat trick of smoke and mirrors Mr Dolby. You did quite well to work that out, although it took you a painfully long time over it."

Zac continued on his own track.

"He obtained the instruments of torture, very risky all of that stuff. So, that was his reward? Like your brother, totally expendable?"

Mrs MacManus again laughed shrilly.

"Yes expendable! He fetched the packing case from the castle and provided the tools to do the job. So what? That was simple enough. A child could have done it. He forced my weak-willed brother into the stocks, but it was I who stuffed-up his stupid mouth. He helped me with the fat landlord too, and with that idiot Brydson. I threw enough suspicion onto him with his own opinion of you Sassenachs to put the police on the wrong trail. That worked damned well. None of you are especially clever are you?"

Zac kept cool.

"What about the forgeries ma'am. You not telling me you believe you're a real queen? Britain has a queen. Queen Elizabeth the Second of the House of Windsor. She's up there in the castle right now."

On the plinth the crazed woman waived her hand imperiously.

"What does that matter? As Scotland follows its own destiny there'll be a new order. In this life you take what you want lieutenant. That's what royalty's always done. That's what I'm doing now!"

I thought loyalty came with the job of royalty ma'am?"

"Only until the final moment of triumph Mr Dolby. Now's that moment. Now is also the moment for this useless English policewoman to die."

Abbi cried out in fear as the blood-streaked knife used to slay Duncan Dewer was raised up tight against the pale skin of her neck.

Zac called out loudly.

"Mrs MacManus, a question."

"I've answered enough questions from you Mr Dolby. I'm tired of your crass Bronx accent and your child-like views. You Americans have never had the stomach for blood. Now you'll have to witness your English sweetheart die, and like it."

Gasps came from the captive audience.

Zac calmly:

"Mrs MacManus, what about Scotland's future hopes for independence? What if the Scottish people always vote to remain with the English and the Union? If they choose to stay together, what of your crown then?"

Mrs MacManus fixed him with a devilish eye.

"I've told you Yankee fool. Now is our moment in history, time to relight Scottish ambition. We've waited a long time for this moment. I've played the English game until I was sick to the stomach. Those privileged little Eton brats. When the postman started his petty pilfering, it gave me the cover I needed to steal their wealthy parents' gifts out of the post. It was all blamed on the fool Brydson."

Mrs MacManus teetered on her plinth. She grinned round at the assembled police still holding the knife firmly to Abbi's white, slender neck.

"You idiots! Did you really think I was a nice refined Englishwoman tending to the needs of those wealthy English spawn?"

Abbi screamed…

"Zac!"

The sharp crack of a gun echoed across the Long Walk and out through the black night towards silent old oaks of the Great Park. It also rang out towards Windsor Castle and the Town. Everyone sighed in unison and in relief… It was over.

"Why did it take them so long?"

Zac put his hand on Abbi's arm as he passed her a glass of chilled white wine.

"They had to be sure that you wouldn't move, otherwise you'd have been Abbi jam!"

"Yes thanks lieutenant, I've always admired your crass sense of humour. That's humour with an "ou" by the way."

Zac looked over, concealing his warmth towards her as well as he was able.

"So do you think there's a place for me here in Thames Valley?"

"You'll have to talk to Pawley about that. I'm just a humble DI remember?"

Zac smiled.

"I want to know how the MacManuses kept it from everyone that they were brother and sister."

Abbi thought.

"I suppose they just produced fake paperwork. They must've posed as a childless couple, but as a couple they would still have the credentials to tend to the needs of the Eton Boys. I suppose Tim MacManus was a pretty good history teacher and Mrs Mac-Psycho a damned convincing actress."

"Yes good cake too!

"You know Amy told me just now that they found a discarded red Royal Mail post-cart amongst the rubbish on a service-road at Queensmere. They must've taken the poor swan there in the cart still alive, killed it *in situ* at the scene probably in the cart itself, and then discarded the evidence."

"Jeez... crazy! Did Wylie get back OK by the way?"

"D'you really care detective?"

"Yes I do, as it goes. Sure he's a pain in the butt, but he's the one that cracked the case in a way."

"How so?"

"Well following up on that fruitcake site The Jacobites' Return. If he hadn't taken that seriously we wouldn't have known about the whole fake lineage."

"Yes Zac, but in the end our even more nutcase woman would've come out of the woodwork anyway. She was so convinced she had the right."

Zac sipped at his beer.

"Yeah OK, but look at monarchy, what is it really? It's the rich and powerful taking what they want, and then over time it just becomes like the status quo right? It's not that crazy an idea in itself. Everywhere in the world there are takeovers of sovereign territory."

Abbi play slapped his hand.

"Are you saying that our Queen and our Royal Family are just rich and powerful from plundering, and that's why they are up there in the castle ruling over us?"

"Well sort of."

"Mr Dolby I'll have you know that you're a guest in this country and I could probably ask Her Majesty to revoke your visa this afternoon if I ask nicely."

Zac grinned a wide grin.

But I do like your Queen. She's a good egg!"

His oppo pouted without meaning it.

"Abbi, you know the curry-house thing…?"

Abbi looked over seriously for a moment at her clean-cut American colleague.

"Ok, if you must know. Wylie and I were an item for a short time. And I mean a short time."

Zac waited for her to continue.

"The thing is, which is partly why I bailed out of the relationship, he was always going on about how a policeman would make the best ever killer. He said that if he wanted to do someone in nobody would catch him. He also had a morbid interest in weapons and stuff like that."

"And...?

"Well the thing is when we were having dinner at the curry-house I started thinking about all of it, and I just convinced myself that he could've had something to do with the deaths. I know now that it was pure paranoia."

Zac tried not to smile. Abbi noticed him suppressing it enough to dig him painfully in the ribs.

"I see you're a smartarse Mr Dolby. I may have to discipline you."

"Discipline huh, sounds good! Let's argue about it over dinner shall we? What about that curry-house?"

"No Zac!"

"OK ma'am, just so long as neither of us has to cook. I've seen more than enough knives, culinary or otherwise for one day."

They made their way out of the pub to find a place for dinner in the charming small cobbled streets of the town of Windsor. As he got up Abbi's hand accidently connected with Zac's rear.

"Did you just touch my ass ma'am?"

Abbi smiled at him.

"No, your *arse* Lieutenant, your *arse*, you're in England now!"